SIAM

or
THE WOMAN WHO SHOT A MAN

A NOVEL BY

LILY TUCK

A PLUME BOOK

PLUME
Published by the Penguin Group
Penguin Putnam Inc., 375 Hudson Street, New York, New York 10014, U.S.A.
Penguin Books Ltd, 27 Wrights Lane, London W8 5TZ, England
Penguin Books Australia Ltd, Ringwood, Victoria, Australia
Penguin Books Canada Ltd, 10 Alcorn Avenue, Toronto, Ontario, Canada M4V 3B2
Penguin Books (N.Z.) Ltd, 182–190 Wairau Road, Auckland 10, New Zealand

Penguin Books Ltd, Registered Offices: Harmondsworth, Middlesex, England

Published by Plume, a member of Penguin Putnam Inc. This is an authorized reprint of a hardcover
edition published by The Overlook Press, Peter Mayer Publishers, Inc. For information address The
Overlook Press, Peter Mayer Publishers, Inc., Lewis Hollow Road, Woodstock, New York 12498.

First Plume Printing, November 2000
10 9 8 7 6 5 4 3 2 1

Grateful acknowledgment is made to the following for permission to reprint previously published material:
Selections from *The New York Times*, copyright © 1946, 1949, 1967 by The New York Times Co.
    Reprinted by permission.
Lyric excerpts from "Getting to Know You," "Shall We Dance?" and "Happy Talk" by Richard Rodgers
    and Oscar Hammerstein II, copyright © 1949, 1951 by Richard Rodgers and Oscar Hammerstein II.
    Copyright renewed. Williamson Music owner of publication and allied rights throughout the
    world. International Copyright secured. All rights reserved. Reprinted by permission.
Excerpt from *Thai Style* by William Warren, copyright © 1989 by William Warren. Reprinted courtesy of
    Rizzoli Publishers.

 REGISTERED TRADEMARK—MARCA REGISTRADA

The Library of Congress has catalogued the Overlook Press edition as follows:
Tuck, Lily.
Siam, or the woman who shot a man : a novel / by Lily Tuck.
    p.   cm.
    ISBN 0-87951-732-9 (hc.)
        0-452-28206-3 (pbk.)
    1. Thompson, James Harrison Wilson, b. 1906   2. Vietnamese Conflict, 1961–1975 Fiction.
I. Title   II. Title: Siam.
PS3570.U236S53   1999
813'.54—dc21   99-37832

Printed in the United States of America
Original hardcover design by Bernard Schleifer

PUBLISHER'S NOTE
Although this book contains material from the world in which we live and references to actual people and events, it must be read as a work of fiction.
Names, characters, places, and incidents are either the product of the author's imagination or are
used fictitiously, and any resemblance to actual persons, living or dead, business establishments,
events, or locales is entirely coincidental.

LILY TUCK was born in Paris and lived in Thailand in the early 1960s. She is the author of two previous novels: *Interviewing Matisse, or the Woman Who Died Standing Up* and *The Woman Who Walked on Water.* She has written numerous short stories, the most recent of which have been published in *The New Yorker, Fiction,* and *The Antioch Review.* She divides her time between New York City and Maine.

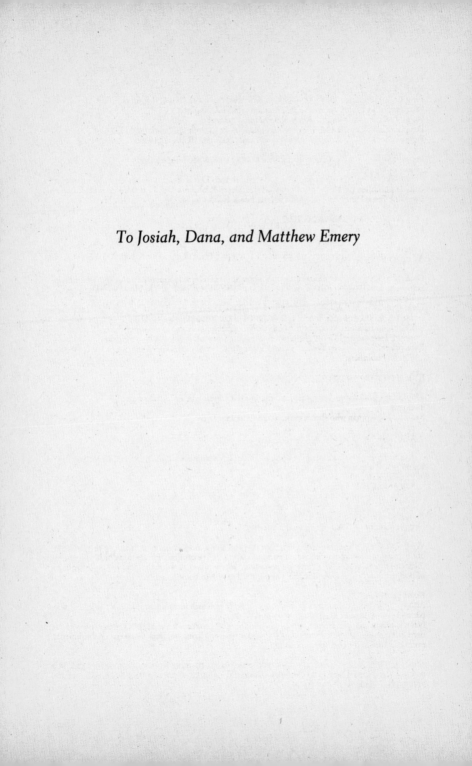

To Josiah, Dana, and Matthew Emery

ACKNOWLEDGMENTS

For generosity in various forms I thank Frances Kiernan.

I am also most grateful to the Sewanee Writers' Series made possible by the Walter E. Dakin Memorial Fund established by the estate of Tennessee Williams.

Innocence always calls mutely for protection when we would be so much wiser to guard ourselves against it; innocence is like a dumb leper who has lost his bell, wandering the world, meaning no harm.
—GRAHAM GREENE, *The Quiet American*

We wish the School Mastress to be with us in this place or nearest vicinity hereof to save us from trouble of conveying such the lady to and fro almost every day also it is not pleasant to us if the School Mastress much morely endeavour to convert the scholars to Christianity than teaching language and literature etc. etc. like American Missionaries here because our proposed expense is for knowledge of the important language and literature which will be useful for affairs of country not for the religion which is yet disbelieved by Siamese scholars in general sense.
—from a letter KING MONGKUT wrote to Anna Leonowens

PROLOGUE

CLAIRE AND JAMES FLEW FROM BOSTON TO Bangkok on their wedding night. The flight took nearly twenty-four hours, and since they were flying at night, west, the plane never caught up with the sun. The whole time it stayed dark.

The plane, an old Air America turboprop, was filled with soldiers. Not all fighting men, James had explained to Claire, but men like himself who worked for JUSMAAG, for USOM and USAID, men who were affiliated with a branch of the armed forces or who had contracts with government agencies. Except for the stewardesses, Claire was the only woman on the plane.

Somewhere over the Pacific, Claire could not say at what time exactly—each time they landed to refuel, she had to keep putting her watch forward, first two hours, then three, then three more—or in what place exactly—maybe over the island of Wake or further south, over the island of Guam— James pulled out the armrest between their seats, covered them both with blankets, and made love to her. Afraid that a soldier seated across from them or a stewardess walking up and down the aisle might see them, Claire did not move.

James appeared not to notice—it excited him to do things differently.

No sooner had James and Claire met, no sooner had they finished their first meal together than they were in bed. Claire had the impression that she was swallowing the last morsel of food, wiping her chin, digesting still. From then on, too, it seemed as if they were always in bed: in the backseat of a car, in a locked toilet, pressed up against clothes and scattering shoes in a closet, once on Claire's parents' antique four-poster while Claire's parents were away. Several times a day Claire raised her skirt, dropped her pants. Her fingers, too, learned to unzip, to unbutton with the swiftness and skill of a lacemaker. It was not how Claire had imagined it, but there was hardly time for anything else.

Coincidentally, James and Claire met on an airplane. "Is this seat taken?"

Absorbed in her book, Claire barely looked up. During the short flight she could feel James watching her. Although it was still winter in New England where Claire lived, James was remarkably tanned.

"What's your book about?" he finally asked.

Claire blushed. She was reading *The Wilder Shores of Love.*

"Basically I'm a soldier," James told her. "Joint United States Military Assistance Advisory Group. I'm lucky, Thailand's not a bad place to live. Everyone's so friendly, everyone's always smiling. And you should see my house—hot and cold running servants, a pool, a garden filled with—"

"But isn't it dangerous? I've read that Chinese commu—" Claire's voice was vague, her words drowned out by the noise of the landing gear being lowered. She did not even know where Thailand was.

"It's pronounced *tie* not *thigh* land." James reached over and touched Claire's lightly. "And the Thais are on our side." His voice was naturally loud. "Besides the word *thai* means free. Speaking of free—how about you? Are you free for dinner?"

Claire hesitated. She clutched her book. She was not used to making quick decisions.

"Come on," James said, taking her arm. "Where's your spirit of adventure?"

When at last the plane landed in Bangkok, it was bright day. They had crossed the international date line; they had lost a day entirely.

James put his arm around Claire's shoulder. Despite the long flight, he appeared rested. "We made it," he said.

Thighland.

No. *Tieland.*

Claire had hardly slept, and her feet were so swollen that she could not put her new red shoes back on. She had to walk barefoot across the hot Thai tarmac holding the new red shoes in one hand. Looking up at the blue sky, she half expected to see the lost day, resting on a bank of clouds, float slowly away and out of her reach.

"We've lost our first married day," she told James.

The lost day was Thursday, March 9, 1967. The same day on which Prime Minister Thanom Kittikachorn first announced to the Thai people that United States aircraft were bombing North Vietnam from bases in Thailand.

1

"Do you know Prajnaparamita?" Jim Thompson held up a small bronze statue with a dozen arms. He spoke as if he were introducing Claire to one of his close friends. "She's the goddess of wisdom. And this is Chanda-li." Jim Thompson picked up another bronze statue from his desk and handed it to Claire. "She's a goddess, too, a yogini. She's the destroyer of ignorance."

The statues were solid bronze and heavier than they looked. Claire held a statue in each hand, weighing them. "Of the two, Chanda-li has the harder job," she said.

"You're quite right," Jim Thompson answered, taking Claire's arm to guide her back to rejoin his guests.

In the drawing room, the sofas, the chairs, the cushions, the low carved Thai teak bed—which served as both table and seat—were covered in silk: yellow, green, orange, red, violet, blue silks. On the side tables, delicate lacquer bowls held macadamia nuts, pistachios, sunflower seeds. Bencharong vases were brimming with jasmine, roses, and tuberoses. Their sweet scent filled the air.

Dressed in a bright sarong, a barefoot servant walked

quickly past on the polished wood floor; he was balancing a tray of drinks—iced water, whiskey, champagne.

"The house is open to the public twice a week, like a museum," Claire overheard a woman say.

"I've heard that Jim's collection of Southeast Asian art is one of—" someone else started to answer as Claire moved away.

The drawing room opened onto the terrace. Past the garden of long-leaf mangoes, arching rain trees, fragrant frangipani bushes, on the other side of the canal, like a lit-up scene set in a play—a play performed expressly for them—Claire could see the silk weavers spinning and dyeing their bright skeins of threads. Intent on their work, the weavers did not look up.

"Beautiful, isn't it?" Claire said when James came up and put his arm around her. "Jim Thompson told me that when he first arrived in Thailand there were only about a dozen silk weavers—just a cottage industry, he said."

"Yeah, and it's been profitable for him, too." James squeezed Claire more tightly to him. James was broad shouldered and strong. He had curly red hair. Every morning, he combed it down with water, but by afternoon his hair had sprung back into bunches of tight curls—worse, in Bangkok, James said, because of the humidity. "What do they call him? The Thai silk king."

Claire was seated next to a Thai prince and a brigadier general. The brigadier general was the first to speak. "Tell me, how long have you two been married, Claire?" He hesitated slightly when he said her name.

"Two weeks." Claire blushed.

"This must be quite a change for a pretty young woman like you. Have you known Jim Thompson long?"

"Just tonight."

"Jim and I date back to the war—the Second World War. We were in the OSS together—the Office of Strategic Services. You weren't even born probably."

Claire looked over at Jim Thompson who was sitting at the head of the dining-room table. In his late fifties or early sixties, blue-eyed, his light hair receding, Jim Thompson looked like a lot of men—bankers, lawyers, her father's friends, her mother's relatives, neighbors. Sensing perhaps that Claire was looking at him, Jim Thompson glanced up, smiled at her. But his good manners, his politeness, had struck Claire right away. She smiled back. More than politeness, there was an innate courtesy, a gentleness about him—the way Jim Thompson had taken Claire's arm and guided her through the rooms of his house.

The Thai prince told Claire that he had studied at Harvard.

"My father teaches at Harvard," she said.

The Thai prince smiled. He had even white teeth. He spoke with a British accent. "What does your father teach?"

"Classics."

The Thai prince shook his neat dark head. "I'm afraid I did not have the pleasure of studying with your father. I went to the Harvard Business School. But I did study Latin as a boy. I can still recite a great deal of the *Aeneid* by heart: *Arma virumque cano—*"

Claire nodded. *"Troiae qui primus ab oris—* And what do you do?"

"Cement. I'm in the cement business."

"And how do you know Mr. Thompson?"

"I've known Jim since the war actually, when he first arrived in Thailand, during the reign of King Ananda."

"King who?"

"Our present king, King Bhumibol's, older brother. King Ananda was killed in a most unfortunate accident."

"I'm sorry. I didn't know."

"Very few foreigners do. I'm afraid foreigners don't take much interest in our history."

"I was planning to—" Claire started to say, but the Thai prince had turned away to talk to the woman on his other side.

Claire helped herself a second time to a dish of tiny shrimp cooked in a sauce flavored with lemongrass that was neither too hot nor too spicy. She admired the blue and white china off which she ate, the grace of the servants who handled the plates. Bouquets of purple orchids decorated the table; the silk napkins, the silver, the glasses all gleamed in the candlelight. The night air was fragrant with frangipani blossoms and the women's perfume.

The woman on Jim Thompson's right was dressed in silver; the star sapphires at her throat reflected the light. She held one of Jim Thompson's hands in both of hers, and whatever she was telling him made him laugh. The woman on Jim Thompson's left had bright red lips and fingernails painted to match; her thick dark hair was coiled elaborately around her head like snakes. She was leaning lightly against him. The coils brushed Jim Thompson's shoulder, and she, too, was laughing.

"Jim has many good friends in Thailand." The Thai prince had followed Claire's gaze. "My wife is especially fond of him."

Nodding, Claire wondered which of the two women was the Thai prince's wife—the silver one or the one with the snakes? And which wife?

Across the table, James sat next to the French cultural attaché's wife. Like Claire, the French cultural attaché's wife was blond, but she was plumper. James, too, was making her laugh. When the French cultural attaché's wife leaned over, James could look down her low-cut dress.

"I hope you will have a chance to visit other parts of Thailand," the Thai prince was saying. "There are so many beautiful places—the ancient capitals of Ayuthaya, of Sukhothai." Before Claire could answer—her mouth was filled with a delicate mixture of mangoes and coconut milk—the Thai prince said, "Your husband, I imagine, has to travel a great deal."

The brigadier general turned to Claire and asked nearly the same thing: "How often does James have to go up north? Where does he go? Korat? Udorn?"

"Nakhon Phanom. James goes once a week."

"James may have to go up more often now. Between the communist insurgents and the North Vietnamese, life is not getting any easier for us."

"I read in the paper about the peace talks—" Claire started to say.

"If only it were so simple—but you shouldn't be worrying your head over such things." The brigadier general patted Claire's arm. "Anyway, it's not our problem. It's Bob McNamara's problem."

Jim Thompson's cockatoo was perched on the terrace railing. As Claire walked back to the drawing room, the big white bird raised the bright orange crest on top of his head and whistled. Without thinking about it, Claire put out her arm to him. Right away the cockatoo clambered onto it. His sharp claws dug into her flesh as, balancing himself with his strong black beak, he climbed up her arm. Once the cockatoo had reached Claire's shoulder, he lowered his head next to hers. She could feel the soft brush of his feathers against her cheek.

"He wants you to scratch him." Jim Thompson was standing next to Claire. "Right there under his crest."

Cautiously, Claire reached up and did.

"He's a smart bird. He likes you," Jim Thompson said. "Most people are afraid of him. My houseboy, Yee, won't go near him."

During coffee, Jim Thompson, James, and the brigadier general sat out on the terrace; they smoked cigars. "In the past," Claire heard Jim Thompson say, "Thailand was able to keep its independence because it was able to maneuver, to take sides without making a commitment—as in the case of the Japanese. But this is no longer true. The American presence in Thailand has eliminated any hope that the Thais can negotiate and reach any kind of agreement with their neighbors—Burma, Laos, Cambodia, Vietnam, even North Vietnam. In other words, to put it crudely the way we do down in Delaware, the Americans have Thailand hogtied."

On the way home in the Land Rover, James said, "You made a big hit with Jim Thompson and that parrot. I was afraid it was going to take your arm off."

"I liked him—I mean Jim Thompson—and I liked the cockatoo. Maybe we could get one."

"Cockatoo? Over my dead body—those birds give me the creeps." James pulled Claire over closer to him on the car seat. "What did you and Prince Chamlong talk about? He's supposed to be one of the richest men in Thailand. His wife is related to Prime Minister Thanom."

"*The Aeneid.*"

"The what?"

"I don't know. King Bhumibol's brother, King Ananda." Claire yawned, still unaccustomed to the different hour, to the different day. "Tell me again how you know Jim Thompson?"

"Bangkok's a small—" James suddenly braked the Land Rover. "Did you see that? Doesn't the idiot know how to signal!— Jim Thompson? Everyone knows Jim Thompson."

"Jim Thompson said he would show me the rest of his house when he got back from his trip to the Cameron Highlands. I liked Jim Thompson," Claire said again, putting her head on James's shoulder. "I liked him."

2

V ENICE OF THE EAST WAS HOW CLAIRE'S GUIDEBOOK had described Bangkok, and Claire and James's house was on a canal, a *klong*. The *klong* led to a large outdoor market called Pratoo Nam; Claire could go there by boat. From the terrace of the house, Claire could hail a boat, like a taxi, and pay only a *baht* or *tical*, which rhymed with nickel—its worth. The taxi boat was a slender hull of teak with an outboard engine, and a propeller shaft so long that the boatman had to lift it out of the water to avoid other boats, refuse, whatever else was floating in the canal. Often a dead dog floated in the canal. Bloated, brown, pink, black, and terrible, the dog bobbed up and down gently, ready to burst.

The other passengers in the taxi boat were slender Siamese women wrapped like parcels in their pink, blue, yellow sarongs. They ignored the dead dogs, and, unless the boat became unusually crowded, they avoided sitting next to Claire.

Falang falang—foreigner, foreigner—the women said to one another in their sing-song voices—*falang falang*.

At first Claire did not venture far into Pratoo Nam. The

market was large, and she was afraid of losing herself amongst the mangoes, the papayas, the litchis, the pineapples and coconuts, the limes piled almost as high as she, the twenty-six varieties of banana, the fish, the squid and octopus from the Bay of Siam, the spinach leaves, the bunches of onions, the clumps of garlic, the live poultry and the hundred-year-old black duck eggs soaked in horses' urine. She was unaccustomed to the sweet cloying scent of jasmine and tuberoses, the pungent strange spices, the rancid smell of frying sauces.

Bpai nai?—Where are you going? The vendors called out after Claire.

When the vendors saw Claire, they doubled their prices. Twenty-five, tall, blond, Claire was easy to see. She wished she was less conspicuous; she wished she was petite and dark with folding limbs like their maid, Noi.

The first time Claire bought a chicken, she had not known how to say *gai*—chicken—in Thai; she had not known how to bargain or say *kill, pluck, and clean it*. She brought the chicken home, flapping and squawking in her basket, and James had to kill it.

"I'll show you how," he offered.

"Poor old *gai*," she answered. "I can't stand the sight of blood."

But Claire watched as James chopped off the chicken's head. She watched as he cleaned the chicken easily. James hunted and he was used to dead things.

Later Claire helped James pluck the chicken. She threw the feathers and the other offal into the canal. But at dinner that evening nothing James said could convince Claire to eat the chicken.

"*Pok pok pok.*" James could imitate animal sounds, the sounds of machines stopping, starting, guns going off, bombs dropping. James smacked his lips. "Delicious."

All their food was prepared in a hot pepper sauce by the cook, Lamum. "The peppers kill the parasites," James said. He was proud that he ate local food and was not sick from it. The food burned Claire's mouth, her throat, her stomach, later her ass. With her chopsticks Claire picked at her meal, shoved aside the peppers, the seeds. "The smaller they are, the hotter," James warned her. Claire's plate was a mess.

"Remember the dish we ate at Jim Thompson's dinner party?" Claire asked. "Shrimp in a lemongrass sauce? Maybe Lamum could cook us something like that."

"Go ahead and ask her," James answered.

The kitchen was the home of ugly water rats. Claire had seen Lamum throw a piece of burning charcoal at one. The pots and cooking utensils were kept in a screened cupboard; the legs of the cupboard were set in pans of water so the ants could not crawl up. There were no appliances; the stove was two charcoal pits. There was no sink; the cold water from a single spigot ran directly onto the cement floor.

"Is Lamum Noi's mother?" Claire asked James.

"I have no idea."

"They don't look at all alike. Noi is so pretty. I like Noi better."

The maid, Noi, had a baby boy. Except for a silver net that he wore over his penis, the baby boy was always naked. He was frightened of Claire, of how she looked—blue-eyed and blond. If he saw Claire, he started to cry. At night, to put him to sleep, Noi masturbated him.

"Is the baby Prachi's?" Claire also wanted to know.

Each time Claire went around to the back, where the kitchen was and where Lamum, Noi, and Prachi, the house-boy, slept, there was always somebody else, somebody new, somebody she had never seen before. A cousin? An aunt? A younger brother? As far as Claire knew, she and James

were supporting an entire family, an entire village. And
hadn't she once seen a horse back there? Or had she only
dreamt this? It was best not to ask. It was best not to get
involved, James said.

The back of the house looked like a jungle. The banana
trees with their large messy leaves and all the garbage Lamum
and Noi collected—empty bottles, wire hangers, tin cans. And
all the laundry was put out to dry there. Not just James's shirts
and socks, her skirts and blouses, but everyone's underwear—
James's, Claire's, Prachi's, Lamum's, Noi's—all together.

A different place, the front of the two-story white stucco
house was neat. The mowed green lawn, the bougainvillea,
the frangipani, the rose bushes. Claire had planted the rose
bushes herself, but because of the heat or the bugs—she
could never tell which—the roses did not do well. Claire was
lucky if one bud bloomed.

The swimming pool, too, was in front of the house.

"We are not naturally immune the way they are," Claire
told James about the water. She and James drank bottled
water. Once a week Noi carried two cases of the bottled water
up to their bedroom. Noi climbed the stairs two at a time
holding a heavy case easily under each arm.

From where James and Claire sat every morning having
breakfast, they could watch a woman bathe in the canal. First
the woman brushed her teeth, then the woman soaped her
face, her neck, her arms, she soaped underneath her sarong.
When she was finished, the woman pulled a clean sarong on
top of the old sarong, without exposing any bare flesh.

"All these months and I still haven't seen her tits,"
James said.

"I don't understand why they're not all sick," Claire went
on to James. "I don't understand why they're not all dead.
That water is indescribably filthy."

Each morning, too, Noi washed her baby boy in the canal. First she rinsed out the silver net, then she held the baby boy up above the canal so that he could defecate into it.

"It's full of shit," Claire said.

James put down his coffee cup, looked at his watch. "I've got to go to work," he said.

3

ONCE A WEEK JAMES FLEW TO NAKHON PHANOM TO supervise the construction of runways. When she first arrived in Thailand, Claire wanted to go to Nakhon Phanom with him and see, but James told her that the airbase was off limits to civilians; also he talked about the lack of accommodations. Claire, he said, could not stay with him in the officers' quarters; she would have to spend the night in a Chinese hotel in town. The Chinese hotels were dirty; they had no sanitary facilities.

"The toilets, they're nothing but holes in the floor," James said, "and there's not much to see in Nakhon Phanom anyway. The northeast of Thailand is the poorest part of the country. So poor that the guys digging a ditch alongside a new runway for me last week were digging with wooden hoes, while right next to them lay six brand-new American steel shovels. It took me a few minutes to figure out that you can't use a steel shovel if you're not wearing shoes."

"I see," Claire said. She did—she saw cut-up, bleeding, bare feet. Still she tried to persuade James. "That way I could picture you when you're away."

James was not persuaded. "It could be dangerous."

"Dangerous how?"

"Guerrilla bands. Insurgents."

"What sort of insurgents?"

"Communist insurgents."

And across the Mekong from Nakhon Phanom was Laos.

"*Louse*," Claire said.

"No," James corrected her, "*Lay-oss.*"

During the first few weeks in Bangkok, Claire was busy fixing up the house: she sewed cushions for the rattan sofa in the living room, she bought woven grass mats to cover the stained wooden floors, she repainted the bedroom walls white, she bought hangers for their closet, put up shelf paper, hung a mirror in the bathroom.

Also Claire took Thai lessons.

Cow cow cow cow—rice? nine? old? come?

Every afternoon during the hottest part of the day, when the house was shuttered and still, Prachi, Lamum, Noi, and the baby boy with the silver net over his penis were napping, the green grass of the lawn was burning, the garbage in the stagnant canal out back was floating in place and stinking, and outside their gate, the drivers in the half-dozen samlors parked in the lane were slumped over their wheels asleep, Claire was sitting at the dining-room table opposite slender Miss Pat trying unsuccessfully both to stifle a yawn and to shape her mouth for the five different tones in the Thai language.

All five tones sounded alike.

Mai pen rai—nevermind—Miss Pat urged Claire to try again. Miss Pat was patient; Miss Pat did not perspire; Miss Pat did not dream of lying in bed upstairs reading a book or leafing through a magazine; Miss Pat always smiled.

Mai mai mai mai—not, new, burn, wood.

The five tones, Miss Pat explained, are: the midtone which is pronounced flat—*mai*; the low tone which is pronounced at the bottom of the vocal range—*mai*; the falling tone which is pronounced as if one is emphasizing a word or calling out to someone—*mai*; the high tone, the most difficult for foreigners, pronounced near the top of the vocal range—*mai*; the rising tone pronounced like the inflection given to a question—*mai*.

To make sure that Claire understood, Miss Pat drew a little graph with arrows, like notes, rising and falling or shooting straight forward, representing the five different tones.

Mai mai mai mai—Miss Pat made Claire repeat.

Prachi spoke more English than either Lamum or Noi did. If Claire wanted to tell Noi something—for instance that her ironed blouses should be hung on a hanger while James's shirts should be folded inside the drawer—she had to tell Prachi first. Prachi would then translate for Noi or for Lamum what Claire said. At the beginning, however, Claire made a point of trying to explain to Prachi in Thai how to hang up James's khaki pants with the creases pressed exactly together, how to achieve the high polish James insisted upon for his black shoes, or how to do something with the swimming pool.

Prachi saaht sa wai nam dai mai?

To clean the pool properly, Claire told Prachi, he had to fish out the leaves that had fallen into it from the frangipani tree and bougainvillea and he had to pour in the chemicals. And Prachi, as if he really meant to do his best to understand what Claire was saying in Thai, would rock back and forth on his dark callused heels, nod or frown for all he was worth.

Chai chai.

Still, to Claire, the pool always looked dirty. "Filthy," she said. The water was coated with a green slime. The green slime was hard to describe, but it was pervasive; it was getting into her hair. "James, haven't you noticed the color my hair is turning?" Claire asked.

"You have beautiful hair." James wound a blond strand around his finger. "I love your hair."

James would swim in the pool at night after dinner. He did not really swim; he floated on his back and looked up at the sky, at the stars. He tried to coax Claire to get into the water with him.

O, *Clair de ma lune,* he sang out to her.

Where else would she have her own pool to swim in? James called out in the dark to Claire. Where else would she have a frangipani tree outside her bedroom window? Where else would she not have to lift a finger to do housework? From where Claire was sitting on the terrace, she argued that a swimming pool was not everything, and she could never get used to the heat, the humidity, the *pricky noo* in the food— the hot little peppers that were named after mouse drop- pings. And what about the china sauceboat that had belonged to her grandmother? Claire had brought it with her all the way from home. Had James forgotten already? When the sauceboat disappeared, Claire looked everywhere in the kitchen. A woman she had never seen before was squatting in front of the charcoal burners heating water for tea. The woman frightened Claire—her mouth was black and filled with betel nut—and Claire had not understood a word the woman said when she told her what she was looking for.

Sossbowt, the woman repeated.

"You know what else I found out, James?" Claire asked from where she was sitting by the pool in the dark. "If the lock under the bridge at Pratoo Nam Market is open, I can go by boat all the way down to Jim Thompson's house."

"I thought he was away," James said, kicking a little in the water.

"I mean when he gets back. Where are the Cameron Highlands?"

"In Malaysia—a popular resort up in the mountains. A lot of rich Chinese own houses there; it's cooler. Why do you ask?"

"No reason. I just wanted to know."

The other thing that James said he was thinking about while he was floating on his back in the swimming pool and looking up at the stars was how he would sleep a whole lot better at night while he was in Nakhon Phanom, if there was a man in the house. Ideally a man and a dog—only Claire was allergic to dogs, wasn't she?—to protect her against the thieves, the *kemoy*, who made a habit of robbing the rich foreigners, the rich *falang*. All the *kemoy* had to do was slash the window screens with a knife and walk right in.

From where he was floating in the pool, James made the sound of a screen being slashed with a knife.

"James, don't!"

To Claire, Prachi did not look strong enough. Neither, to her mind, did Prachi look tall enough. He was not as tall as she was. But it was plain that Prachi was agile. Claire had stood in the garden with Noi one day watching Prachi use a plaid cloth to climb up the trunk of a coconut tree with his bare feet, doing it almost perpendicularly. Yes, Claire had to admit that Prachi was wiry, and that when Prachi leaned over with his net to fish the bougainvillea and frangipani leaves out of the pool, she saw on Prachi's back a whole set of muscles she never noticed James had.

The other thing Prachi could do was open a Coca-Cola bottle with his teeth—the sound it made was the sound of a tooth breaking. But Prachi had straight perfect white teeth, and like most Siamese, Prachi smiled a lot. Prachi smiled even when there was no reason to.

At night James could fall asleep instantly—the instant he finished making love to Claire, the instant he rolled off her, he was fast asleep, his mouth open, snoring a little—but Claire could not. At full speed the electric fan over their teak bed with its kapok mattress—kapok was cooler, James said—sounded like the engine of a jet plane. In the dark Claire would strain to listen beyond the noisy fan for the sound of thieves. With their curved and razor-sharp knives, they were preparing to steal from them—the intrusive foreigners—if need be they were preparing to slash their throats as well. Maybe Prachi, Lamum, maybe even pretty, graceful Noi had told them. If Claire dared, she would have gotten out of bed. She would have gotten James's loaded gun, the Smith & Wesson. Instead she raised her head slightly off the pillow, looked out the window past the frangipani tree that grew lush and fragrant and assumed night shapes, to the house next door. The balcony of the house next door was crowded with orchids in varying stages of bloom, forced to grow there by a neon tube which stayed lit all night. Often Claire would count orchids, like sheep, before, finally, she fell asleep.

4

"*Tow rai?*"—HOW MUCH? CLAIRE ASKED THE SAMLOR driver. She was on her way to meet James and Siri for lunch. She gave him the address of the Chinese restaurant.

"*Yee sip baht,*" the driver answered.

"Ten," Claire said.

They settled on fifteen, and the samlor driver set off swiftly. He swung out of the lane into the larger avenue, Sukhumvit, without looking. Claire did not look either. Better not to, she had decided. Better to be oblivious to the Bangkok traffic, better to pray or to cross her fingers. In the open cab she felt completely exposed. Her bare legs pressed tightly together, Claire hung on to the leather strap as the driver maneuvered in and out of the larger cars, trucks, buses. Like most Thais, the driver believed in predestination. Should he have an accident, it was fate, not his fault.

"*Cha cha*"—slow slow—Claire said from the backseat. The words sounded ridiculous, mere ritual. The driver nodded his head to show that he had heard her, but he did not slow down. Claire no longer expected him to.

Thailand is divided into seventy-one provinces called

changwats. Each changwat has a governor appointed by the Ministry of the Interior. These changwats are further divided into amphurs and there are four hundred and eleven amphurs in Thailand and each is governed by a nai amphur. In the sam-lor, Claire tried to read.

She was learning about the population, the crops, the history. Claire had to concentrate. Most of the books were dull, factual, out of date. An English major, she was more accustomed to novels. In school she had learned how to pick out symbols, metaphors, how to analyse a text, and, to her, the struggles between the Siamese, the Burmese, the Laotians, seemed like meaningless bloodbaths; the migratory routes appeared random, accidental. The Thai history books were as thick and as impenetrable as jungle, the texts as dense as if they had been written in hieroglyphics or Greek. But Claire should have been used to that—after all, her father was a professor of classics. Even so, her father would be no good in the orient. Near-sighted, he would trip over bamboo, step on a snake. Claire's mother, on the other hand, would fare better. She was practical. *Where exactly are we?* she would ask.

So far on the trips with James to the beach, to Hua Hin and Siracha, to the ancient capital of Ayuthaya, the roads were full of potholes, washed-out bridges, detours; often even the road disappeared. The signs along the way were written in Thai and indecipherable. Not easily put off, James would stop the Land Rover, ask someone for directions: *How far? Klai*—near? *Klai*—far? The word in Thai was the same, but pronounced in the midtone? the falling tone? the rising tone? A good mimic, James was learning how to speak Thai fast, while, in vain—*klai klai klai*—Claire searched for Miss Pat's graph. In each village James would find the *nai amphur*. The *nai amphur* would invite them to his house. James and Claire

would take off their shoes, sit cross-legged on the floor on
bamboo mats. In honor of the occasion, the *nai amphur*
fetched his bottle of American Scotch. Claire hated the taste
of whiskey, but she had to drink up, to the last drop; she had
to show the *nai amphur* and upturn her glass. More than the
whiskey, the remoteness of the village disturbed her. James,
on the other hand, was not afraid. He liked to discover out-
of-the-way places.

"It's bound to change soon," he said. "Westernization.
Roads. In a couple of years, you'll see, Claire, all these villages
will be full of backpackers, hippies, tourists."

In the Chinese restaurant, Siri ordered the food: roosters' testicles and ducks' gelatinous feet. Claire would have preferred
something else—plain rice—but Siri did not consult her. Siri
did not look at her. Siri's slanted eyes were nearly hidden by
his jowls. Siri was huge. Siri was half-Chinese. Toward James,
he made a point of being westernized: he slapped James on
the back, he used outmoded American expressions. "You
betcha," Siri said to James as he grabbed for the testicles, for
the feet.

Both men loved to eat.

"I met Siri when I was first stationed in Thailand. Siri
sort of picked me up," James explained when Claire asked
him what Siri did. "Siri knows a lot of government
officials, customs officials. He can arrange for export licenses,
hunting licenses, all kinds of stuff. Siri's a useful friend
to have."

"I guess," Claire said.

"The first night, Siri took me on a tour of the nightclubs
on PatPong Road. I drank so much Thai whiskey—boy, that
stuff is potent—I can't remember a whole lot about the
evening, except for this one thing."

"What was that?" Claire asked.

"The expression on a soldier's face when a ping-pong ball bounced out of a woman's vagina and landed on his lap at the Pink Elephant Club."

"A ping-pong ball?"

"Even if I live to be a hundred years old, I swear," James continued, "I'll never forget that soldier's face—the soldier was in a wheelchair. Poor bastard."

"Poor woman," Claire said, but James was no longer listening to her.

In the Chinese restaurant, his mouth full of slippery food, Siri started to tell James how he had read in the newspaper that a well known American millionaire had disappeared without a trace in Malaysia.

"American who started Thai Silk Company," Siri said.

"You mean Jim Thompson?" Claire asked. "That can't be. What paper?"

Siri took a Thai newspaper out of his briefcase. "You see, picture of him." Siri pointed to an article on the front page.

Claire looked at the photograph of Jim Thompson holding a piece of silk cloth between his outstretched hands. "Read it, Siri. What does it say?"

"Let me see," James said.

"But we had dinner with Jim Thompson just ten days ago, just two weeks ago."

"Newspaper says that Jim Thompson, American silk king, has been missing since yesterday. Mr. Thompson who is sixty-one years old was visiting friends in Cameron Highland resort in Malaysia. Friends of Jim Thompson, Dr. and Mrs. Ling"—Siri was reading haltingly, translating word by word, guiding himself on the page with a fat finger—"antique dealers. Another friend, Mrs. Connie Mangskau, also antique dealer here in Bangkok city, said Mr. Thompson had gone to

sit outside house after lunch, all others went inside house."
Siri paused, looked up at James and Claire.

"Yes. Go on," James said.

"Soon after 3 P.M. same friend, Mrs. Connie Mangskau
from Bangkok city, said she heard sound of chair being
moved on verandah, then sound of footsteps going down
gravel path. She thought, she said, footsteps were Mr.
Thompson's and that he was going for a walk. Later his suit
coat was found on back of chair and his cigarettes and some
pills he took for pain of—" Siri hesitated, stopped.

"Pain of what?"

Siri shrugged and put the newspaper down. "Newspaper
says Jim Thompson probably lost in jungle. But not true. Not
lost in jungle."

"What do you mean, Siri?"

"Jim Thompson not lost in jungle," Siri repeated. "Jim
Thompson seized by communists. Chinese communists very
smart people. Communists very bad people."

"Communists? How do you know? Does it say communists in the newspaper, Siri?" Claire asked.

"I heard the same thing," James said. "I heard that he
may have been kidnapped."

Claire turned to James. "You didn't tell me."

"I heard it this morning at work. But I heard that the kid-
nappers were ordinary thieves—*kemoys*, Siri. *Kemoys* who
wanted to rob him or kidnap him for ransom. After all, Jim
Thompson's a rich man. Jim Thompson's a millionaire."

"Siri, what does your newspaper actually say? That Jim
Thompson went for a walk after lunch? That could mean
anything. It could mean he got lost or he fell down or—"

"No, not *kemoys*, communists. All Thai newspapers say
so. Communists, I know," Siri said again.

"But, Siri, aren't all the newspapers and radio stations in

Thailand owned and run by the government?" Claire started to ask. Even while she spoke, she knew that no matter what she said—*What about freedom of the press? What about freedom of speech?*—Siri's response would be the same. He was not listening to her.

"Thailand always a free country, free from communism. Communist people very bad and America our friend," like a refrain, Siri said to James.

"For a price," Claire muttered to herself before she gave up. It was no use discussing with Siri.

"Does it say anything else?" Claire took the newspaper from Siri and looked at Jim Thompson's picture again.

"They're bound to find him," James said. "I heard that they're going to send down a bunch of Special Forces guys—those guys have dogs and all kinds of heat-sensitive and radar equipment. Claire, aren't you hungry?"

Claire shook her head. "Why would the communists want to kidnap Jim Thompson?" she tried asking again.

"Speaking of equipment, Siri, remember how I was telling you about the single-barrel forty-millimeter anti-aircraft—" But already James was talking to Siri about something else.

Claire had never held a gun. Until she met James, Claire did not know the difference between a rifle and a shotgun. James owned several. He owned a pistol, too. A Smith & Wesson .44 magnum. It was his favorite and he liked to handle it, spin the cylinder, cock it. He kept the gun in a bureau drawer by his side of the bed. "I'll let you get the feel of it," he had told Claire. "I'll show you how to fire it." The Smith & Wesson .44 magnum was heavy. "A handgun is different," James had also explained to her. "You shoot from the hip; you don't aim. You shoot instinctively. To kill." Claire had held the gun in both hands. "You look at the largest area of the body, like the chest. Not the head," James continued. "That way you have less chance of missing. And with these bullets you are bound to stop him. They explode on impact. They make a hole as big as my fist."

Stop whom? Whom was James talking about? Claire had handed him back his gun. She might shoot it. Pulling the trigger looked easy, as easy as turning a page in a book. More than a hobby, guns were James's passion. "I'll show you how," he had said again.

"Claire? Hello, are you listening?" James startled her.

"Sorry. I was still thinking about Jim Thompson," she said. "You didn't finish, Siri. Medicine for what sort of pain?"

"I don't know word in English." Siri pointed to his large side.

"Liver? Kidneys?"

"No, not liver, not kidney." Siri shook his big head. He turned back to James. "You like to swim, James? You like beach, James? Thailand has many beautiful beaches. One day you come and visit me in my house in Pattaya. You meet my wife."

"Your wife? That would be nice, Siri."

James gave Claire a sharp look. Sarcasm was a cheap shot, and wasted on the Thais. They did not understand it. There was no word for sarcasm in the Thai language.

"I'd love to meet your wife, Siri," Claire said, ignoring James.

She would. Probably, Claire imagined, Siri's wife was beautiful and unhappy to be married to Siri. At this very moment she was plotting her escape with a lover, a childhood sweetheart, a slim young man from her village.

"And one day I go visit you in Nakhon Phanom, James," Siri was saying. "I go look at your runways, James."

James shook his head. "Sorry, Siri, I've told you already, they're off limits. Off limits to civilians."

"Why? Are runways paved with gold?"

"Yeah. Paved with American dollars."

A duck foot was caught in her mouth. Claire could not swallow it. When Claire started to choke, James slapped her on the back. In the restaurant, the people at the next table stopped talking, looked over at her. The waiters, too, stared as James pounded Claire's back.

"I'm sorry," Claire was finally able to say. "I can't eat this. Could I have plain rice instead, Siri?"

5

"WAT PHRA KEO WAS BUILT BY KING RAMA I FOR Emerald Buddha. Emerald Buddha is most sacred image in all of Thailand. Emerald Buddha is guardian of independence and prosperity," the guide said.

Claire had joined a tour group made up of other JUSMAAG officers' wives. They met once a week.

"A good way to meet people. A good way to see Bangkok," James said.

"Next I'll be drinking gin and playing mah-jongg all afternoon," Claire answered him.

James poked Claire in the ribs. "And you'll get fat."

"Is the Emerald Buddha really made out of an emerald?" a JUSMAAG officer's wife wanted to know.

"Emerald Buddha discovered inside pagoda near Chiang Mai when pagoda struck by lightning," the guide went on, ignoring the JUSMAAG officer's wife's question. "Later, Laotian invaders stole Emerald Buddha from Chiang Mai. Laotians took Emerald Buddha to Luang Prabang. During reign of King Taksin, Emerald Buddha brought back to Thailand, to new capital in Thonburi, across Chao Phya River, by General Chakri who succeeded Taksin as Rama I."

Claire took a deep breath and asked, "Was King Taksin the king who was beaten to death with sandalwood clubs because no one was allowed to touch him?"

"Taksin great king. Taksin expelled Burmese from Thailand."

Two JUSMAAG officers' wives were standing together talking. "My husband heard a report that a kidnap band has been operating in the Cameron Highlands and holding wealthy Chinese for ransom," said the first.

"I read in *The Bangkok Post* that the police think he was dragged off by a tiger or a man-eating leopard," said the second, making a face.

"I met Mr. Thompson. I had dinner at his house just a few days ago." Claire had gone over to where the two women were standing. "I can't stop thinking about him."

"Come along, ladies." The guide motioned to Claire and to the others.

"Strange isn't it? And you'd think Jim Thompson's new store on Suriwongse and Rama IV Road would be deserted," the second woman went on. "Instead it was crowded with tourists. Tourists who'd read about him in the papers."

"What did you buy?"

"Four yards of turquoise plaid silk."

"Please, ladies, take off shoes. We will go inside temple now. Three times a year, at beginning of each new season, King Bhumibol himself changes Emerald Buddha's robes. For hot season, Emerald Buddha wears—"

"Hot? You can say that again." The first woman made a fanning motion with her hand.

"—a golden diamond-studded robe. For rainy season, Emerald Buddha wears—"

"Where did you say Jim Thompson's new store was?" Claire went back and asked the women. "Suriwongse and what road?"

"Rama IV."

Verbs in the Thai language have a single fixed form, Miss Pat said. Verbs in the Thai language are not conjugated according to person or tense. The context usually makes it clear whether it is the past, present, or future. If, however, one has to be specific, a time-marker word is added. There is no difference between adverbs and adjectives in the Thai language, and adjectives can be used as verbs, Miss Pat also told Claire.

"A woman with a gun brings bad luck," the hunter told James in Thai when he saw Claire get out of the Land Rover.

In English, to Claire, James said, "Bullshit. Don't pay any attention." James pulled a hundred *baht* bill out of his pocket. "He's just saying that to get more money."

The hunter, a wiry, short man, was barefoot. He wore only a *pakama*—a plaid cotton cloth wrapped around his waist and twisted between his legs. He carried a machete. Loaded down with packs of food, guns, ammunition, James and Claire tried to keep up with him. They walked single file, with Claire last.

Claire slipped and slid in the paddy mud. From time to time she sank nearly up to her knees in it. With each step her shoes oozed, sucked, and made farting noises. She tried to stay within James's diminishing shadow; she tried to step on James's back; as the sun rose, to step on James's head of curly red hair.

"Damn," Claire muttered to herself. She was carrying the shotgun barrel down the way James had shown her. A twelve-gauge, the gun was too heavy for her. The wooden stock was wet with her sweat; Claire kept shifting the gun awkwardly between her hands. She had tied her hair back, but she had forgotten to bring a hat. She had a kerchief, but the kerchief was red and not camouflage, and James said she should not wear it. The sun beat hot on her head. The rice paddies shimmered all around, and an occasional palm tree marked a distant point on the dazzling, almost yellow horizon.

Two boys were tending water buffalo, they were sprawled naked on top of the buffalos' backs. When James and Claire walked by, the boys sat up. "No eye contact," James had warned about the buffalo. "They hate how we smell." Claire looked the other way—the water buffalo might charge her.

"*Falang falang*"—foreigner, foreigner—the two boys jeered.

"*Ling Thai*"—Thai monkey—Claire mumbled back.

A few minutes later, four or five railbirds flew up from almost under their feet. James took aim. With two shots he hit two birds. Too late, too slow, Claire missed them completely. The recoil of the gun was so unexpected she nearly cried out. She had no idea that it would be so painful—a hard punch.

Like a bird dog the hunter plunged into the paddy water. Nearly swimming, he retrieved James's shot birds. One of them was still alive. The hunter wrung the bird's neck.

Midday they stopped at a small hummock of land with a few bamboo houses on it. The houses were on stilts, the roofs thatch. Laundry was hanging out to dry, but no one was about. A few scrawny chickens scattered under the houses as they arrived. The hunter left them.

"Where did he go?"

"I don't know. To take a pee."

"Maybe this is a trap," Claire said.

"A trap for what?" James put his arm around her shoulder. Still sore from the recoil of the gun, Claire shrugged it off.

"I don't know. To rob us."

Holding two glasses of tea, the hunter returned. He gave both glasses to James.

"See," James said as he handed Claire one of the glasses. "Stop worrying all the time."

While they were eating their lunch, the villagers appeared and formed a semicircle around them. The villagers were so quiet that, at first, Claire did not see them arrive. She looked up from her ham sandwich, and suddenly there they were. About twenty of them—men, women, children— crouching on their heels and watching James and Claire eat.

Then their hunter stood up. His Thai was colloquial and Claire understood only the word *falang* which he repeated often. The hunter told the villagers the story of James and Claire: how they had arrived in the heavy Land Rover; how they had walked all morning in the rice paddies; how James had shot the railbirds. The villagers listened intently. Claire glanced over at James. Finished with his lunch, James was lying on his back, his hands clasped behind his head. The two shotguns were lying next to him, broken. Before they had sat down James had removed the shells. *Ping*, the hunter was saying for James's gun going off. *Ping, ping.* He fired at make-believe birds in the air. The village men stood up. Holding make-believe guns, they raised their arms, volleyed. *Ping, ping, ping.* Then James stood up. *Bang*, he said, joining the make-believe shooting. *Bang, bang.*

"*Mem*," a woman called out as Claire got up to leave. "*Mem*." The woman was holding out a straw hat.

Claire shook her head.

"Claire, take the hat, or she'll lose face."

"That's a lampshade, not a—" Claire started to argue with James. "What should I give her—my red kerchief?"

Later that afternoon she shot her first bird.

"I got him!" Claire shouted to James. Elated, she did not notice the recoil of the gun.

"Bull's-eye! You sure did."

When the hunter retrieved the railbird, there was nothing left of it. The railbird was a bloody pulp—not even worth keeping to eat. The hunter shucked it back into the rice paddy.

The railbird Claire shot had chicks. The hunter found three of them and tied their feet together. He would take them home, he told James, raise them to eat. Swinging upside down from his *pakama*, the baby railbirds looked pitiful.

"The aborigine hilltribe people who live in the Cameron Highlands are friendly and more likely to help than to hurt a lost man." On the way back in the Land Rover, Claire was reading aloud from a newspaper article. *"Police officials continue to dismiss rumours that Thompson has been kidnapped. They appear to be working on the theory that he was dragged off by a tiger or other wild beast—* Oh, God, what do you think, James? About Jim Thompson. Do you think he was kidnapped or dragged off by a tiger? James?"

"I don't know. I'm driving. A wild beast."

"Although the Cameron Highlands are well laid out with many trails for hikers, closing in on every side is one of the most impenetrable jungles in the world."

"No kidding. Tom McNeal—we work together, you haven't met him yet—told me how a few weeks ago they just found the wreck of a U.S. Air Force C–47 that crashed in that same jungle area way back in 1947. The plane crashed a few miles from the main road. That was twenty years ago." James said.

"Police officials speculate that Jim Thompson may have

wandered off the trail and lost his way," Claire continued.
*"Brigadier General Edwin Black, Commander of United States
Support Forces in Northeast Thailand*—James, that's the man
I sat next to at Jim Thompson's dinner party—General Black!
He said he was an old friend of Jim Thompson's. He said he
knew Jim Thompson from World War II, from when they
were in the— Oh, look, James!"

From a distance the two elephants on the road looked
like a mirage. The men sitting on top of them were prodding
them along with sticks, kicking them rhythmically behind the
ears. The elephants moved quickly on their thick legs.

James blew the horn of the Land Rover.

The elephants' ears flapped like huge moth wings as they
passed each other on the road. The men on top of the elephants ignored the Land Rover and the sound of the horn.

"At a press conference held today," Claire resumed reading aloud from the newspaper, *"Brigadier General Edwin
Black was quoted as saying: 'A body is different. A body should
not be hard to find in the jungle. Vultures fly over it. Animals
are attracted by the smell.'"*

"Yeah, no kidding," James said again.

After they returned from their hunting trip Claire tried
to give the straw hat to Noi. Instead of smiling—smiling
the way she did when Claire gave her other things: an empty
perfume bottle, a plastic container, a cardboard carton something had come in—Noi turned red in the face.

Claire had to ask Prachi: "What's the matter with Noi?
Did I offend her?"

The hat, Prachi explained, was a peasant hat, a hat worn
by people who work outside in the paddy fields. Noi worked
inside a house. Noi would never wear a hat like that.

6

Suriwongse Road was filled with the sound of horns, shouts, the scream of brakes. Cars changed lanes without signaling or warning. Samlors, bicycles, pedestrians, maneuvered hurriedly out of the way. An overloaded bus careened down the street, last minute passengers clinging to the running boards, to the fenders. Trucks rattled by, their exhausts worn. A black Mercedes driven by a chauffeur honked and made its imperious, mysterious way—the windows were curtained and shut. The sidewalk was crowded with food vendors; the smell of fried bananas, pancakes, noodles thickened the hot air. People dodged and bumped into Claire; a group of schoolgirls in their blue uniforms giggled at the sight of her. In front of Claire a man was carrying a big fish on his shoulder. The fish was a shark. Squatting on the sidewalk and holding a child in her arms, a woman tugged at Claire's skirt as Claire walked by. The woman was chewing betel nut. The woman opened her black mouth—*Haar haar*.

Inside the Thai Silk Company bright tidy bolts of material gleamed on the shelves. Noon, the store was nearly deserted, except in the back where a woman was unrolling a large bolt of red silk. The woman shook the red silk until the cloth fanned out in front of her on the wood floor; she leaned over to examine it. She took down another bolt of darker red silk and unrolled it so that it, too, fanned out next to the first red bolt. Claire watched as the woman stood and contemplated both silks for a moment. Then, making up her mind, the woman took out a pair of scissors and made a notch in the darker red silk; swiftly and expertly she tore off a long strip.

"Can I help you?" The woman who had been cutting the bolt of silk spoke with a French accent.

"Mr. Thompson, the owner—is there any news?"

The woman shook her head wearily. "*Non*," she answered. "Are you a friend of Jim's?" She pronounced his name *Jeem*.

"Yes, well, I've met him. We—my husband and I—had dinner at his house about two weeks ago."

"Ah, you went to *Jeem's* house. Beautiful, isn't it? My husband, Anton, and I were on the same plane to Penang, with *Jeem*. We saw *Jeem* just a few days before he disappeared," the woman with the French accent volunteered. "A—how-do-you-say in English?—*coincidence*. My husband, Anton, is a reporter for *The Bangkok Post*."

"Do you think Mr. Thompson got lost in the jungle?"

"*Jeem* might have gone for a walk and fallen; *Jeem* might have broken his leg, broken his *heep*."

"You must have seen him every day. You must have known him well."

"Everyone liked *Jeem*. *Jeem* was a very kind man. Only *Jeem* was a bit absentminded. *Jeem* was always losing his glasses, his cigarette lighter, his *sings*. So, perhaps, *Jeem* was not *sinking*, *Jeem* was not looking where he was going."

"I see." Claire did—she saw Jim Thompson lying helpless at the bottom of a deep hole, his legs broken.

"I'm looking for material for a dress," Claire answered when once again the woman asked if she could help her.

"What sort of dress?"

"I don't know. A dress to go out in. Out in the evening, I mean."

The woman studied her. "With your coloring I would choose *bleu*. Yes, definitely, for you, *bleu* would be lovely."

"No, red. I want to buy red silk." All of a sudden, sure, Claire pointed to the bolts still on the floor. "The red over there. A dress in this silk." She picked up the darker bolt of red silk—the same bolt the woman had cut a notch into and torn a strip from—and held it up to herself in front of a mirror.

"Also I will never forget how *Jeem* was holding a plant in his lap during the flight to Penang," the woman continued, as she measured out the yards of red silk. "He told Anton he was taking the plant to his friends, Dr. and Mrs. Ling. The plant was a Javanese Dendrobium. Lucky, too, because the flight was very bad, very bumpy."

"A what kind of plant?"

"A Javanese Dendrobium. A very rare orchid. An orchid which only blooms once every few years and only for a few minutes. *Jeem* would not let the stewardess put the orchid plant in the overhead compartment—the plane was going up and down so much. The orchid, *Jeem* told the stewardess, was very delicate, very expensive."

When Claire left the half-light of the Thai Silk Company and went out into the hot blue-green of the noisy Bangkok afternoon, she was holding the package with the red, the blood-red, silk tightly in her arms.

Jeem, Jeem, she repeated to herself.

Nii raka thao-rai?—How much is this?

Met la thao-rai?—How much per meter?

What kind of material did Claire have in mind? Silk? Miss Pat wanted to know when Claire told her she was look- ing for a dressmaker.

"Silk. Yes, of course," Claire answered her.

Outside the JUSMAAG headquarters on Petchburi Road, soldiers were playing volleyball on the lawn. When they saw Claire walk through the gate, they began to whistle.

"Hey, blondie!" one soldier called out to her. "You want to be my little sweetheart!"

"How much? A hundred *baht*? Too much!" Another sol- dier shouted after her.

"Don't they have anything better to do?" Claire said to James about the soldiers. She had gone to get money from him for the silk dress.

"Like shine their shoes? Clean their weapons?" James ran his hand through his hair. Midday, his red hair had started to curl. "How much do you need? Is five hundred *baht* enough?"

Claire unwrapped the package with the silk. "Look, James, isn't this lovely?"

"Red? Mmmm, I like red." James put his arm around Claire's waist. "Red is sexy." He put his hand inside Claire's blouse.

Claire pulled away. "No, not here."

As Claire was leaving James's office a soldier came in. The soldier had something covering part of his face. A paper bag.

"Have you met? Sergeant McLean. My wife, Claire."

The sergeant shook his head and put out his hand.

Claire stared. "Oh. You're sick?"

"I've been having a little trouble breathing lately," the sergeant answered from inside the paper bag.

"Time for you to go home, Tom," James said.

* * *

The British Library was located two blocks south on
Suriwongse Road, and was quiet. The only sound was the
sound of pages turning, the whirr of the overhead fans;
few people went there. Each time Claire stopped in, the
librarian, who was from Australia and who looked to be about
Claire's age, would glance up from what she was doing
and say:

"Hot. Never felt so hot in my entire bloody life."

At the beginning Claire imagined that the librarian might
become her friend. First Claire asked her about Australia—
which part she was from. Another time Claire asked her how
long she had been living in Bangkok. Both times the librarian
answered in a whisper: *Melbourne* and *Two and a half years*,
but she did not reciprocate with questions of her own. Instead
she asked Claire if Claire would get her husband some
American cigarettes from the PX.

In return for the American cigarettes, the librarian let
Claire take the magazines home for as long as Claire wanted
to—glossy English magazines with articles both about people
Claire did not know and about plants and flowers that did
not grow in Thailand. A week, two weeks, the librarian said it
did not matter as long as Claire returned them eventually. All
the magazines were out of date anyway. They arrived by sea
mail. Besides, what difference did it make when one planted
bulbs or what one bought for one's fall wardrobe? In Bangkok
there were no seasons—no tulips, no jonquils—and, as far as
clothes were concerned, it was so humid and hot, the librarian whispered to Claire, she wore as little as possible.

"Don't worry, I'm sure they'll find him," the librarian said
when Claire brought up Jim Thompson. "I'll never forget the
time my husband and I got lost near Chiang Mai. We were
walking up this hill, actually the hill turned out to be more
like a bloody mountain, bloody Mount Everest."

Sitting in an armchair, a man was reading *The Guardian*; at a nearby table two English girls were doing schoolwork; books were piled high on Claire's desk.

King Rama IV, also known as King Mongkut, was the first Thai king to try to bridge the gap between the new and the old. He believed in westernization and for this reason hired the teacher, Anna Leonowens to teach his children how to speak English. A gifted astronomer, King Mongkut successfully predicted the total eclipse of the sun on August 18, 1868.

King Nang Klao, King Mongkut, King Chulalongkorn . . .

The unfamiliar names made it hard for Claire to concentrate. Sometimes she skipped a couple of pages.

King Mongkut's son, King Chulalongkorn ascended to the throne when he was fifteen years old. As Rama V, he ruled Siam for forty-two years. During that time, he changed his country from a backward land to a . . .

In spite of herself Claire's mind wandered. She pictured a jungle, a bamboo jungle. The bamboo grew so tall and thick that it took more than the hunter's machete to cut through it. The bamboo jungle was full of wild animals, snakes, dangerous carnivores. She pictured a shinbone, or a larger bone, a pelvis picked clean of meat uncovered in a man-eating leopard's lair.

During King Chulalongkorn's reign, Siam was forced to surrender Laos and Western Cambodia to France. Siam also had to cede part of the Malay Peninsula to Britain. The price of maintaining peace and independence.

Again Claire's mind could not stay on the text. She pictured a pair of prescription sunglasses, the lenses miraculously still intact, a Zippo lighter wrapped in vines and lianas, discovered in the deepest part of the jungle by an aborigine. The sunglasses fit him and the lighter still worked. The flame lept up and burned the aborigine's finger.

Claire turned to the next chapter:

King Vajiravudh, King Chulalongkorn's successor, encour-
aged women to keep their hair long; he encouraged them to
replace their dhotis with the panung, a Thai-style sarong . . .

7

THE GUIDE POINTED TO A SIXTH-CENTURY LIMESTONE
torso of the Buddha standing in Jim Thompson's garden.

"Dvaravati style," he said.

Purple orchid plants were placed around the statue.

"Brad, *mah* husband, swears he was kidnapped," a
JUSMAAG officer's wife with a southern accent said. She was
standing in the black-and-white marble entrance hall of Jim
Thompson's house. "Kidnapped *foh* ransom. Apparently he
maid a fortune with the Thai silk business."

"Mr. Thompson's house was assembled from five old
Siamese houses," the guide said, leading the group of
JUSMAAG officers' wives up the stairs. "Please, take off
shoes," he also told them before continuing. "Oldest part,
drawing room, is from weaving village of Bang Krua; second
oldest is kitchen wing, once part of palace; master bedroom
and dining room come from houses in Pak Hai and were
brought down to Bangkok on barges; cook's house is from
Banglampoo, a district in Bangkok. Only part of house that is
not from Thailand is carved wall between drawing room and
master bedroom. Wall was entrance to Chinese pawnshop."

"I met Jim Thompson, I knew him," Claire was saying again. This time she was talking to the JUSMAAG officer's wife who spoke with the southern accent. "James and I had dinner here less than a month ago. Hard to believe, but I was standing right where you're standing now, talking to him."

In the drawing room, the chairs, the cushions covered in yellow, green, orange, red, violet, blue silks, the low carved Thai bed that served as both a table and a seat, the lacquered side tables on which stood delicate bowls filled with flowers—roses, jasmine, tuberoses—looked the same. To Claire nothing seemed to have changed.

Again the barefoot houseboy, dressed in a bright sarong, hurried noiselessly past them on the polished wooden floor.

The guide pointed out the statues in the room: a large U–Thong-style head of the Buddha; a pre-Angkor head of Suriya, the sun god; an eleventh-century limestone head of Siva; a statue of the half-male, half-female Ardhanari; a Khmer-style statue of Hari-Hara; a statue of Siva and Uma and their bull, Nandi. And against the far wall, two wooden Burmese statues of spirits called *Nats*.

Then the guide led the group of officers' wives out onto the terrace. The terrace, he explained, was paved with seventeenth-century brick from Ayuthaya which had been brought down as ballast in the rice boats. Beyond Jim Thompson's garden and across the *klong*, the guide pointed to the weavers, who were sitting on the floor of their open-frame wooden houses, spinning the silk, and who again, intent on their work, did not look up. They were used to tourists visiting Jim Thompson's house.

"Funny, the weavers were spinning the same pink plaid the time I—" Claire started to say at the same time as the guide called out to them, "This way, ladies. Next we visit Mr. Thompson's dining room."

The walls of the dining room were covered with silk paintings. The silk paintings depicted the legend of Prince Vessantara. According to the legend, the guide explained, Prince Vessantara had to give up his wife and children, his house, all his possessions, to attain perfection.

"Many legends have grown up around actual painting of Vessantara Jataka paintings. One legend says that painter will die if he completes a set. As result, a painting is always left unfinished—house without roof, tree without branches, branches without leaves."

The dining-room table was set for eight. The blue and white Ming china, the silverware and crystal, the red silk napkins were all in place.

"I was sitting here," Claire told the woman with the southern accent. "In this very chair."

"Mr. Thompson was well-known host. Famous people from all over world attended Mr. Thompson's parties. Isn't that right, Yee?" The guide turned to the houseboy in the bright sarong, who was squatting near the door listening to the guide, and who, as if accustomed to this, stood up and repeated the names of Jim Thompson's famous guests:

"*Sassy Peeton, Dloomang Gaboady, Lowbut Kangeely, Samset Maw, Eder Meiman, Bhala Hootong*—"

"Oh, by the way, *mah* name's Deirdre," the woman with the southern accent told Claire.

"Mine's Claire."

"Do you have any theories about what happened to Mr. Thompson?" another JUSMAAG officer's wife was asking the guide.

"Mr. Thompson had many competitors in Thai silk business. Perhaps someone from another company, a rival company, was jealous," the guide answered her.

"What did Jim Thompson look like?" still another

JUSMAAG officer's wife wanted to know. Then a third asked, "How long did you say he'd been living in Bangkok?"

"He promised to show me around his house," Claire was telling Deirdre as together they walked into the next room. "It's hard to describe but I can still feel the way he held my arm— Oh, look, there's Prajnaparamita and there's Chandali, she's a yogini and the destroyer of—"

"Please, not allowed to touch." Just in time the guide stopped Claire from picking up a statue.

Jim Thompson's desk was crowded with a dozen small bronze statues; several Celadon bowls, jars, a miniature rain drum; a pair of scissors and a letter opener in a leather case, pens, pencils. A guestbook covered in printed Thai silk lay opened to a page on which there was a pen-and-ink drawing of a man with a bird perched on his shoulder.

"That's him, I recognize the cockatoo!" one of the JUSMAAG officers' wives cried out. "Cockatoos are supposed to be very smart."

"I've seen pictures of Jim Thompson. People say he was a queer."

"I heard Jim Thompson was working for the communists. The Chinese communists," another JUSMAAG officer's wife remarked.

"How old was he?"

"He just turned sixty-one."

"Where was he from? The south somewhere. Delaware?" All the JUSMAAG officers' wives were talking at once.

"I thought he lived in New York."

"Oh, Jim Thompson. I don't know. I think he was divorced."

"Mr. Thompson's house became such a tourist attraction that Mr. Thompson was forced to open it to public two days a week so strangers would not walk in on him in his bath."

The guide was moving the group toward the next room—Jim Thompson's bedroom—just as the houseboy came up and spoke to him in Thai.

"I am sorry, but Yee says not possible to visit Mr. Thompson's bedroom now. Some repairs are being made. You, ladies, will have to come back and see bedroom another day," the guide also said.

"What sort of repairs?" one of the officers' wives wanted to know.

"Suay suay mahk"—lovely, very lovely—Noi said. She clapped her hands together like a child when she saw the flowers Claire had bought at Bangrak Market—the same kind of flowers that were in Jim Thompson's house: tuberoses, jasmine, pink and white roses.

"Chai chai suay." Claire was putting the flowers in a vase on the dining-room table. From the look of dismay on Noi's face, she knew right away that instead of having said *suay* with the rising tone—lovely—she had said *suay* with the falling tone—ugly.

The flowers came wrapped in a newspaper, a Thai newspaper. At the top of the page the name JIM THOMPSON was written in large block letters. Below the name, creased and wet from the flowers, was his photograph—the same photograph Claire had seen in Siri's newspaper.

Looking through James's magnifying glass, Claire studied Jim Thompson's face. His blue eyes were half shut—squinting perhaps into the sun? His nose, his mouth—had he been about to speak? to smile?— Or was that a water stain on the paper? Probably he had not wanted to have his picture taken. Someone had convinced him—good for the silk industry. The photographer, too, had been too talkative, too pushy. *Look up. Look down a little, Mr. Thompson.* He had asked him too many questions: *So how long do you plan to be away in the Cameron Highlands? Now look this way, at me, Mr. Thompson. Are you going on business or pleasure? Cock your head a little to the right. A little more to the right. Tell me, what is your opinion about the little war next door? Is it going to affect the Thai Silk Company? That's right. One more question, if you don't mind—your opinion on the build-up of the U.S. military in Thailand? Perfect. Now, Mr. Thompson, if you could smile, please.* But however long and hard Claire looked at the picture, she could find nothing unusual, nothing peculiar, nothing significant in it.

Pom—Miss Pat showed Claire, touching her hair.

Tar—Miss Pat pointed to her eyes.

Ja mook—nose.

Hoo—ear.

Park—mouth.

At the end of the lesson Claire asked Miss Pat to translate what the Thai newspaper said underneath the picture of Jim Thompson:

"*Mr. Thompson's original investment of $700 and a lot of hard work organizing home weavers—only five looms were in use when Mr. Thompson first arrived in Bangkok—grew into an annual business that exports $1.5 million worth of silk*—

"Oh, $1.5 million is a lot of money," Miss Pat interrupted herself to say.

"—*a business that employs 4,000 people during the peak weaving period. It was also at Mr. Thompson's shop in Bangkok that Queen Sirikit bought several bolts of gold silk that she presented to Queen Elizabeth on a visit to Britain*—

"Queen Sirikit *suay mahk*."

"Yes, Queen Sirikit is very lovely," Claire agreed with

Miss Pat in English as Miss Pat began reading again:

"*The reward in the search for Mr. Thompson who disappeared in the Cameron Highlands was raised to 500,000 baht today—*"

Miss Pat paused and calculated. "Twenty-five thousand U.S. dollars."

"*An alternative reward of 200,000 baht is offered—*"

"Ten thousand dollars," Claire said.

"*—for information leading to the discovery of his body if Mr. Thompson is not still alive. Persons having any information are asked to telephone 55882-3; write to GPO Box 2189; or contact the Thai Silk Company at 9, Suriwongse Road.*"

After Miss Pat had left, Claire cut the photograph of Jim Thompson out of the Thai newspaper and put it inside her top bureau drawer, next to her scarves, her underwear, her jewelry.

"We went to visit Jim Thompson's house," Claire told James later that day. "Everything is the same, the way it was. The statues, the china, even the flowers in the vases. His study. His desk. No one has touched anything. In the dining room the table is set for eight, as if he were expecting us."

"When Jim Thompson first came to Thailand at the end of World War II, he was in the OSS," James said. "God, I'm hot. You want to go for a swim, Claire?"

"The whole time I was in his house I half-expected to see Jim Thompson walk through a door; I half-expected him to come and say hello to us. It was strange. Weird."

"Now people are saying that the reason Jim Thompson disappeared was that he was in the CIA. Come on, Claire, put on your bathing suit."

"It was weird," Claire said again.

8

IN THE MIDDLE OF THE NIGHT WHILE CLAIRE WAS TRYING to sleep, there was a coup—or an attempt at one. The rebels, who called themselves the Revolutionary Party, tried to seize the state radio station. The fighting, a minor skirmish lasting only a few hours, took place in front of Government House off Phitsanuloke Road. The royalist forces had put down the rebels, the captured rebel leader was in government custody. James and Claire read about it the next morning in *The Bangkok Post*.

"Will they shoot him?"

"If he's lucky." Still reading the newspaper, James put one hand up to his head as if he were holding a gun to it. "*Click*," James said, then, "*Bang*."

"Poor man. The paper is biased. Who knows what the facts really are?" Claire sighed. "The truth?"

"It's the same old story. Thanom can't justify martial law forever. Once again we support an undemocratic government in the name of democracy," James said.

"But hasn't Thanom instituted a lot of reforms in Thailand?"

"Reforms are not exactly Thanom's priorities."

"What are his priorities?"

"Oh, Claire." James put down the newspaper. "The official line is that Thanom's priorities are national defense, counterinsurgency, the balance of factional power, and private commercial activities. The unofficial line which happens also to be mine is that Thanom's priorities are his own private commercial activities."

Prime Minister Thanom Kittikachorn, who had been vacationing in southern Thailand, was on his way back to Bangkok. He had declared a temporary state of emergency, a curfew in the streets. In Switzerland the king and queen of Thailand were also curtailing their holiday and returning home. All morning radio announcers reassured the Thai people of the strength and solidarity of Prime Minister Thanom's government. The perpetrators of the coup would be punished; fortunately there had been only a few casualties.

Claire had read about one of them—a young woman. On her way home from where she worked, she had been caught in the crossfire. Alive when she was brought to the Seventh Day Adventist hospital, she died during the surgery to remove the bullet.

"Thai doctors," James said.

"It says here she worked at the Erawan Hotel. That's only about half a mile from here. She was a maid," Claire said.

"A maid?" James rolled his eyes. "A maid in the middle of the night? Give me a break. But in the long run this coup attempt may not be such a bad thing. Thanom has to be careful now," James continued. "Thanom has to prove that his government is stable, otherwise he'll be under more pressure from us to start making some democratic reforms. Nevermind the Rusk-Thanat Communique."

"The *What*-Thanat Communique?"

"Oh, and don't go out today, Claire. Stay home; it's safer," James said.

After James had left, Claire finished reading the rest of the paper: *Meanwhile the local aborigines who still hunt with blowpipes and darts and are thought to be sharp-eyed enough to pick up a man's trail from a broken leaf on the ground, discouraged by their failure to find any trace of the missing Jim Thompson, were returning to their own jungle home.*

Among those who have remained on the scene, however, is Jim Thompson's physician, Dr. Einar Ammundsen of Bangkok, who has postponed his return from a golfing trip in the Highlands. "He is generally in good health," Dr. Ammundsen told UPI reporters about the American millionaire who disappeared over two weeks ago while visiting friends in the Cameron Highlands. "He is susceptible to bronchitis, which would not be good in the jungle. But he is generally in good health."

Prachi, Lamum, and Noi seemed unperturbed by the news blaring forth from the radios along the *klong*. Noi made up the bed, swept the house; in the kitchen Lamum washed rice under the single spigot; Prachi cleaned the pool, putting in the chemicals and fishing out the leaves with the long net the way he always did.

Again Claire was reminded of the maid—except that James was probably right: the maid was a prostitute. She tried to imagine what sort of man—most likely a businessman; the Erawan Hotel was filled with them—she had slept with last. A taciturn Swede? a heavyset German? a slender Japanese? Probably the man would not remember the maid's name or what she had looked like—only that she was clean and in a hurry to get home.

* * *

Dear Mom and Dad . . .
Claire started to write a letter:
Everything in Thailand is fine. James goes up to Nakhon Phanom which is in the northeast once a week (a couple of times he's gone up twice a week), and except for seeing more soldiers around town, you would hardly know anything was going on in Bangkok. The big subject of conversation is the weather! Thank God for the pool. I spend most of the day in it. We have a house-boy whose name is Prachi and whose main job, besides taking care of James's uniform and stuff, is to keep the pool clean. Everyone, including the Thais, is waiting for the rainy season to begin so that instead of it being 100 degrees in the shade (I am not exaggerating, yesterday it was 100.2 degrees, the hottest day in thirty years), it will only be 90 degrees . . .
Claire started again:
Dear Mom and Dad,
Please don't worry about us—the newspapers always make things sound worse than they really are. Bangkok is pretty quiet, except for downtown, but James and I don't get to go downtown or to nightclubs much! I'm taking Thai lessons with a woman called Miss Pat—Pat is pronounced in the midtone otherwise pat would mean eight or goat! Soon I expect to be fluent enough to chat with Queen Sirikit! Also I have joined a group of other JUSMAAG officers' wives to sightsee. So far I haven't gotten to know any of them well— most of them have kids and are pretty busy. The other day we went on a tour of the house of an American ex-pat who has a beautiful collection of Thai art. Actually James and I had dinner with him, and you may have read about him . . .
By eleven o'clock Claire was restless, hot.

Claire had trouble finding the dressmaker's house. She had been there once with Miss Pat. The street on which the dressmaker lived was not paved but dirt. As soon as the rains began, the ground would turn to mud. A wide wooden plank for pedestrians and cyclists ran down the middle of the street. Most of the gates to the houses were unnumbered, and the few existing numbers were in Thai. In addition, all the houses looked alike. When, finally, Claire rang the bell of a house she thought was the right one, no one answered. Claire called out the dressmaker's name; she rang the bell again.

Instead of someone coming to the door, from inside the house Claire heard a man yell:

Kill the gooks! Kill the bastards!

Claire did not right away understand; she thought the man was yelling in another language.

Kill the gooks! Kill the bastards!

In the end Claire asked for directions—the man had frightened her.

The red silk dress had a low-cut back and thin little spaghetti straps to hold it up. Claire showed the dressmaker how she wanted the dress to fit her more snuggly. She pulled at the material around her waist, around her hips.

"Tight," Claire said.

"Okay. *Light*," the dressmaker repeated after her.

The Thai house embodies a complex accretion of symbols and beliefs . . . In the British Library, Claire had set aside the history books and was reading about Thai architecture. *Before building commences, the future resident must consult an astrologer to determine the most suitable month. Once a month has been settled, further calculations are necessary to determine the proper day and time to begin placing the pillars in the ground.*

The posts are carefully selected for strength and smooth-

ness, and often auspicious names like king, diamond, and hap-
piness are inscribed on them. The men who carry the posts to
the site and place them in the holes are chosen
for having auspicious-sounding names, or they are given them
for the duration of the ceremony; among the popular names are
'Phet' (diamond), 'Thong Kham' (gold), and 'Ngoen' (silver).

Both the first and second posts to be raised are decorated
beforehand with young banana shrubs, stalks of sugar cane,
and lengths of sacred colored cloth. Gold leaf is applied to the
top of each post. In some places a piece of clothing belonging to
the male of the household is tied to the first post and one
belonging to his wife to the second.

*Seua chert—*shirt.

*Gahng gayng—*pants.

*Tung tow—*socks.

*Chut wai narm—*bathing suit.

Which piece of clothing, Claire wondered, did Jim
Thompson wrap around the post of *his* house?

When Claire got home Prachi was still cleaning out the
swimming pool.

"Prachi," she called out to him, "have you heard any
more news about the coup last night? I read that they caught
the rebel leader. A young man about your age. I don't
remember his name."

Holding the long net in one hand, Prachi stood at the
edge of the pool facing Claire. He shrugged his muscular bare
shoulders; his face was expressionless.

"I guess you are used to government coups," Claire continued. "How many can you remember, Prachi? *Sawng?*
Saam?"

"Thlee." Smiling now, Prachi held up three fingers.

"But as the crow flies, Prachi, Government House is only

two miles from here. Doesn't that frighten you?"

"Prachi not afraid." Prachi was smiling more broadly. His straight perfect white teeth gleamed.

Looking at the clean water in the pool, Claire decided to go for a swim. She walked toward the house to change into her bathing suit. Over her shoulder she called back to Prachi.

"And what about Thanom? Do you like Prime Minister Thanom Kittikachorn? Do you think he is a good man? A good prime minister?"

"Thanom cares for Thai people." Prachi was no longer smiling.

"Well, you know what they say, Prachi? They say that Thanom's priorities are national defense, counterinsurgency, the balance of factional power, and private commercial activities." Claire was already inside the house; Claire was already halfway up the stairs to the bedroom where Prachi could not hear her when she said, "But you know what *Nai* James says, Prachi? *Nai* James says Thanom's priorities are his own private commercial activities."

9

In the Thai language, Miss Pat explained, the *PH* sound is not pronounced like the *ph* in *phone*, it is pronounced like the *p* in *poor*. The *h* is added to distinguish it from the Thai *p* which is closer to the English *b*. There is no *v* sound in Thai so that *Sukhumvit*, for instance, the road off which James and Claire lived, is pronounced *Sukhumwit*.

L and *r*, Miss Pat continued, are used interchangeably and are often transliterated. A common example is the word for foreigner, *farang*, which is pronounced *falang*. One more thing for Claire to remember, Miss Pat said, words that end with *ch*, *j*, *s*, or *d* are always pronounced as if they end with a *t*. Likewise, *g* and *k* and *b* become *p*.

Kir de goop! Kir de bastalt!

The JUSMAAG officers' wives talked about their husbands. Like James, the JUSMAAG officers' wives' husbands spent a great deal of time away in places like Sattahip, Ubon, Korat, Udorn, Nakhon Phanom. The JUSMAAG officers' wives talked about their children who were either at the local American school or away in the States at school. They talked about their servants—how lazy they were, how much the servants cheated them. They talked about the heat, the dirt. Most of all the JUSMAAG officers' wives talked about how they looked forward to going back home.

"Today we will visit Grand Palace, Chakri Maha Prasad," the guide said.

Chowkree Mawhaw Plusawt, Claire mouthed to herself.

All of a sudden she was aware of how different the JUSMAAG officers' wives sounded when they talked. One was from Texas, another was from the South, Claire herself was from New England. Each woman's accent was like a whole other language.

"Grand Palace built by Rama I, first king of Thailand. Each new king of Chakri dynasty has added to it." The guide waved his arms. "Architecture has many styles."

The gold and mosaic palace roofs glittered blindingly in the sun; they reflected the heat—hot, hotter, hotter still. Claire tried to shut out the JUSMAAG officers' wives' accented voices; she tried to listen only to what the guide said.

"If *accawdin* to Dong, Hanoi's *foah*-point program—" a red-haired woman whose bare arms were covered with freckles was telling another officer's wife.

Compared to the graceful Siamese women in their crisp blouses, their flowered sarongs, the JUSMAAG officers' wives suddenly looked too large, too pale, too messy. Claire could not help but notice the clumsy way the officers' wives trailed after the guide, the way their wrinkled skirts hiked up, the way their sleeveless blouses were sweat-stained and their bra straps hung loose on their white arms.

"This way, ladies. Please, ladies, come along. We are now entering, Chakri Maha Prasad, royal residence—"

Chakree Mawhaw Plasad, Claire said to herself as the woman named Deirdre answered the red-haired woman:

"Brad *sayud* we only bombed the *tahgit* list."

"Most *uh* them don't even *flah* with a full ordnance load," the red-haired woman said.

"Chakri Maha Prasad, royal residence, was built during reign of King Rama V to commemorate hundredth anniversary of Chakri dynasty." The guide raised his voice. "King Rama V same as King Chulalongkorn. King Chulalongkorn founded first schools in Thailand, first post office, first railroad, first hospital in Thailand. Chakri Maha Prasad," the guide went on, "is where King Bhumibol, present king, receives foreign ambassadors, where all official ceremonies, state banquets—" The guide gestured to the JUSMAAG officers' wives who were still talking. "Ladies, if you please, follow me—King Bhumibol and Queen Sirikit live in Chitralada Palace. Chitralada Palace is more modern, more comfortable."

Sheetralawdaw Palace, like a tic, Claire could not stop herself.

"King Bhumibol moved to Chitralada Palace after his brother, King Ananda, died," the guide said.

"King *Awnaw*—how did King Ananda die?" The name was familiar to Claire.

"King Bhumibol's brother, King Ananda, committed suicide," the guide almost shouted; the red-haired JUSMAAG officer's wife was still talking:

"What do they expect, zero *suhvilian* casualties?"

"If you please, step here and look at golden urn. Golden urn contains ashes of all Chakri kings."

"I thought King Ananda's death was an accident." *An unfortunate accident*—wasn't that what Prince Chamlong had said at Jim Thompson's dinner party? Claire moved closer to the guide. "Did King Ananda die here?"

"In Borompiman Hall, behind Forbidden Quarters."

Borrowpiemawn Hall.

"The Forbidden Quarters is where king's many wives lived. Each year now, on his birthday, King Bhumibol gives garden party in Forbidden Quarters. All diplomats and officials are invited."

"Can we go? I mean to Borompiman Hall."

Afterward Claire had a headache from straining to hear the guide speak above the penetrating and accented voices of the JUSMAAG officers' wives. She needed fresh air, she wanted to be alone. Instead of going back with the others, she went over to the Pramane Grounds to watch the kite-flying—just a short walk and she would take a samlor home.

At an outdoor restaurant, Claire found a table, ordered a beer, a *Singha* beer. Then from where she sat, she looked up at the kites—hundreds of brightly painted paper birds, snakes, dragons fluttering against the blue sky, against the glittering gold domes, chedis, and wats. The heavier, longer kites were male; the smaller, faster kites, female. The two kinds of kites fought in the wind for dominance.

Claire did not right away hear someone ask her in English,

"Ma'am, is this seat taken?"

A young man, a soldier probably—he did not look more than eighteen—pulled up a chair and sat down at the table next to Claire. "Hi. I'm William—Will."

"Claire," she answered.

"Nice to meet you, Claire." Will put out his hand. She took it. "Claire, that's a nice name. Claire, you look just like my girlfriend back home."

"I bet you say that to all the women."

"It's true. Let me show you."

As Will signaled to a waiter that he wanted a beer—the

same kind of beer Claire was drinking—he pulled his wallet out of his pocket. He took out a photo, handed it to her.

Claire looked at a picture of a smiling young woman wearing a mortarboard. Except for the long blond hair, the young woman did not look like her.

"She's pretty." Claire handed Will back the photo. "What's her name?"

"Lisa. You're pretty, too, Claire. Beautiful. You really are."

Claire shrugged her shoulder. She did not answer Will.

"Where are you from, Claire?"

"Massachusetts."

"Massachusetts. Hey, I'm from the East Coast too. From upstate New York. Rochester."

Will's beer came and he drank half of it down.

"So," he said looking around, "I thought this was a big market. The guidebook said this was the biggest market in town. I wanted to buy stuff," Will continued. "Local stuff to send back home. To send to Lisa. There's nothing here but kites."

"On Sunday," Claire said. "It's a market on Sunday. A plant market. You could buy Lisa an orchid."

"An orchid?"

"Orientals love orchids." Claire smiled. "Orchids are a kind of status symbol. The more orchids you own the richer you are. Some are very expensive, very rare—orchids that only bloom once every couple of years."

"Once every couple of years? You're kidding me. Who would want a plant that just blooms every couple of years? If I bought a plant, I'd want the kind of plant that blooms every day."

"I agree with you." Claire laughed.

"So, tell me, what's a beautiful woman like you doing in Bangkok?"

"My husband," she answered. "He's with JUSMAAG. He's helping the Thais build runways up in Nakhon Phanom."

"The airbase?"

"What about you?"

"I'm on R and R for a couple of days. I'm just back from Tayninh—ever heard of Tayninh? If you haven't, you haven't missed anything. Tayninh is not a good place to be. No, sir—no, ma'am, I mean."

"Where's Tayninh?"

"A few klicks from the Cambodian border." Will took out a pack of cigarettes, offered Claire one. Claire shook her head. "Hey, let's not talk about Tayninh. Let's talk about something else," Will said, lighting his cigarette. "Let's talk about you. What are you doing tonight?"

"I told you, I'm married." In spite of herself Claire was smiling.

"I thought maybe your old man might be out of town in—where did you say he was stationed?"

"Nakhon Phanom."

"Nakhon Phanom. Nakhon Ratchasima, Ubon, Udorn, Ta Khli, all those places are the same, and you should see the high tech stuff they've got crammed up there. Thailand has turned into a giant aircraft carrier. A buddy of mine was up in Nakhon Phanom last week—or maybe it was Nakhon Ratchasima, I don't remember—and he said there was even a hell of a nightclub there now. A crazy place."

"I wouldn't know. James doesn't talk about Nakhon Phanom."

"James? James sounds like an important guy. Is James a five-star general?"

Claire laughed again. "No, James is just a captain, but James did mention the Pink Elephant Club on PatPong Road if you're looking for a nightclub."

"How about another beer, Claire? On me."

Will was easy to talk to—the way Claire imagined she

would talk to a younger brother. She asked Will questions. Questions about Lisa—what Lisa did: Lisa, Will said, was studying to be a pharmacist. Questions about him—what he planned to do when he got out of the army: Will said he wanted to go to college, then to law school.

When it was time for her to leave, Claire offered to write Will, and Will asked if he could kiss her—kiss Claire good-bye, he said.

"Sure." Claire held out her cheek to Will.

The kiss was so unexpected that when Claire felt Will's tongue, she opened her mouth.

"Today we went to visit Chakri Maha Prasad, that's the Grand Palace," Claire told James during dinner. With her chopsticks she was shoving aside the *pricky noo*—the little peppers on her plate. "Afterward it was so hot I went over to the Pramane Ground. I bought myself a beer and watched the kite-flying."

"A beer? I could use a beer right now." James ran his hand through his curly red hair. "I could use a haircut too."

"What about you, James? What did you do?"

"Oh, Claire, I spent the day the same way I've spent every day this week—figuring out how many more goddamn feet of runway a Republic F–105 Thunderchief needs to land on, figuring out how many extra feet a McDonnell F–4 Phantom needs to take off from."

The little peppers were so hot that if Claire accidentally swallowed one it brought tears to her eyes.

"Sorry, I didn't mean to sound—"

Claire shook her head. "It's okay, James."

"I'm tired, I guess," James said. "Tired of Nakhon Phanom. Do me a favor, Claire. Come over here and give me a kiss."

Geeve me ah kiece.

10

THE BANQUET INVITATION WAS DELIVERED EARLY IN THE morning by Captain Ruengrit's driver. When the car horn sounded Prachi went to the gate. Upstairs in the bedroom James and Claire were rocking back and forth on top of each other—this time Claire was on top of James. Their bodies, covered in sweat, made loud smacking noises. From the bed Claire could look out the window.

"What is it?" she called down to Prachi when they were finished. Not only was Claire's body covered with sweat, it was covered with James's red body hair. Then, "Who is Captain Ruengrit?" she asked James.

"Captain Ruengrit is a captain in the Queen Cobra Regiment. He's celebrating his promotion. God, it's hot. Aren't you hot, Claire?" James got out of bed and went to the bathroom.

Instead of a tub or a shower, the bathroom had a large earthenware jar full of cold water. To wash, Claire dipped a bowl into the jar and splashed herself with cold water. Standing naked in the middle of the bathroom floor—the floor was tiled and slanted so the dirty water drained out—

Claire soaped herself, then she rinsed herself off with more cold water from the jar. It was one of the few times during the day that she felt cool. Truly cool.

Lying on the damp sheets under the noisy ceiling fan while James was in the bathroom, Claire stared at the framed photograph on top of her bureau of her parents holding their skis with snow-covered Mount Washington in the background. The photograph was taken a few years ago. Her parents looked healthy and strong. Her father had his arm around her mother's shoulder, and they were both smiling for the camera. Claire tried to put herself in the picture with them—smiling, too, she would be dressed in her red parka and navy-blue ski pants, her goggles on top of her wool cap. Then Claire tried to imagine herself putting on her skis, brand-new red and white Rossignols with Salomon bindings, and getting on the chair-lift. Claire tried to imagine taking a fast run down the mountain—the snow hard, icy in patches—and afterward, to warm up, Claire tried to imagine herself going inside the crowded ski lodge for a cup of hot chocolate, but she could not do it.

In the Thai language, there is a difference between the polite and the popular vocabulary, Miss Pat said. Claire would use the polite word *thaan*, to eat, while her houseboy, Prachi, would use the word *kin*. An altogether different vocabulary called *kham raatchaasap* is used exclusively for the Thai royal family. Claire, for example, would not use the word *thaan* in a conversation with a member of the Thai royal family, she would use the word *rapprathaan*.

Chun thaan gai—I eat chicken.

Prachi kin cow—Prachi eats rice.

Queen Sirikit rapprathaan—but what does Queen Sirikit eat?

The chances of Claire's having to speak to King Bhumibol or to Queen Sirikit, Miss Pat admitted, were slim.

The next time Claire went to the dressmaker, she had no trouble finding the house. The red silk dress fit Claire perfectly—in fact, the waist was so tight she had to hold in her breath while she pulled up the zipper—and the dressmaker only charged Claire the equivalent of twenty dollars.

In the street outside the dressmaker's house a crowd of people had gathered around a man wearing an elaborately embroidered black shirt, a black hat, a heavy silver necklace. Holding the brown paper package with the dress in it carefully so as not to wrinkle it, Claire went over to look.

Claire had seen hilltribe people before at the markets— Meo, Karen, Lahu, Lisu, Akha, even the elusive Phi Thong Luang, "the Spirit of the Yellow Leaves." They sold plants, herbs, amulets. One time Claire had bought a rose bush from a woman whose headdress was made entirely of silver coins, Indian rupees. Claire had tried to bargain, but the woman would not. "Akha," James said. James claimed he could tell the different hilltribes apart. "The Meo or Hmong," he told Claire, "are the most independent; they also wear the most silver around their necks. The Karen men cover their backs and chests with blue tattoos. The Lahu weave baskets . . ." Claire was a little frightened of the hilltribe people—of how they looked—but she admired their jewelry.

The hilltribe man was holding a gibbon in his arms. The gibbon was only a few weeks old. The gibbon had a collar around its tiny beige neck; the collar had bells attached to it. Each time the gibbon moved, the bells jingled and the people watching laughed. The hilltribe man held out the baby gibbon to Claire, and someone called out something she did not understand. Gingerly, she touched the gibbon on the head. The fur felt very light and cottony, the skull as thin as glass. The hilltribe man was smiling and nodding as the crowd pressed in on her. Claire was vaguely aware of trying to hold the package with her new dress in it as far away from her as possible at the same time that the hilltribe man placed the baby gibbon in her arms.

The gibbon weighed nearly nothing. He lay quietly with his head against Claire's chest. Looking up at her with his pale blue eyes, he wrapped his small black hands around Claire's neck. The hilltribe man held up his fingers, naming a price, the same price Claire had paid for the dress.

By the time Claire reached home in a samlor, the baby gibbon had shat on her—a yellow liquid filled with mucus—and had bitten her. The baby gibbon's teeth were like needles, and Claire's arm was bleeding.

After what seemed like an unusually long time—was Prachi sleeping? was Prachi drinking? or had Prachi gone deaf all of a sudden?—Prachi finally opened the garden gate. He was smiling—Prachi was always smiling, smiling when there was no reason to—as he took the baby gibbon from her. Prachi shook the baby gibbon in the air so that the bells attached to his collar jingled. He held the baby gibbon in such a way—by the scruff of the neck—that the baby gibbon could not turn around and bite him.

Suay—Noi made a face as she took the package with Claire's new dress in it. During the trip home in the samlor, the brown paper had gotten torn. Inside the package, Claire could see, the dress was stained with gibbon shit and blood.

When James got back, the shiny black shoes he wore to work were caked with mud—Prachi polished James's shoes until he could see his own face in them—and his khaki trousers had mud stains on them as well. A Continental Air Service plane had crashed during takeoff in Nakhon Phanom, James said. The American pilot, the Thai copilot, and one Laotian crewman were killed. The plane, a Dakota, had been on a regular cargo flight. Before the rescue party had time to get there, the flames had consumed the aircraft and the three men inside it. James had been one of the men in the rescue party, and now he was really beat. He wanted nothing to do with Claire's baby gibbon. If pressed, he would go upstairs and get his gun and shoot the damn thing.

"I mean it," James said. "Gibbons are notoriously mean and spoiled, and this one, I bet, is no exception. He's going to crap all over the house and bite everyone."

When James saw Claire's arm, he insisted she go get a tetanus shot. "Claire, don't you have any common sense?" He sounded angry about it.

The waiting room of Dr. Ammundsen's office on New Road was filled with people—sailors, mostly. Dr. Ammundsen had just returned from Malaysia, the receptionist informed Claire in a whisper. In addition, a Danish ship had come in a few days ago, and she would have to wait. "Will they never learn?" the receptionist continued, glancing at the sailors and shaking her head. "Thank God for penicillin."

Claire said, "No, I'm here to get a tetanus shot."

In his slow, careful English, Dr. Ammundsen, a tall, pale Norwegian, told Claire that, probably, the bite would heal quickly—only in this climate one should never take anything for granted and there was no point taking chances. When Claire raised her sleeve so that he could give the injection in her arm, Dr. Ammundsen told Claire to take off her blouse.

"My husband and I had dinner in Jim Thompson's house

a few days before he disappeared," Claire said, unbuttoning her blouse. "You were his doctor, weren't you?"

"His doctor and his friend." Dr. Ammundsen gave the needle a little preparatory flick with his finger.

"I read in one of the newspapers that he forgot his pain medicine. Medicine for what? Jim Thompson wasn't sick, was he?" Claire felt self-conscious sitting half naked on Dr. Ammundsen's examining table.

"Gallstones."

"Oh, gallstones. Where are gallstones?"

"Gallstones can be very unpleasant, very painful, but gallstones are not life threatening," Dr. Ammundsen said, sticking the needle into Claire's arm.

Claire looked away from the needle. "Do you think there's still a chance of finding him?"

"Not in the jungle. The only hope we still have is if someone comes forward and asks for ransom money." Dr. Ammundsen removed the needle from Claire's arm. "So tell me, young lady, what do you do with yourself all day? Do you play bridge?"

"Play what?"

"Bridge."

Claire shook her head and reached for her blouse. "No. No, I don't."

"Do you play golf?"

"Golf?" She repeated. She was tempted to laugh. "No, I don't play golf either."

"A good-looking young lady like you has to do something to keep busy in the tropics, otherwise—" Dr. Ammundsen's voice trailed off.

"I read a lot." Claire avoided Dr. Ammundsen's eyes as she buttoned her blouse. "I'm reading about Thai history."

* * *

James telephoned Siri the next day. Siri, James predicted, would get rid of the gibbon. James was right. Siri knew someone who raised gibbons. The baby gibbon, Siri promised, would have a good home. Siri also refused the money Claire tried to offer him for his trouble. He or, at any rate, his friend, Siri told her, was the person who was benefiting.

Prachi put the baby gibbon inside a cardboard box for Siri to take away. The box had air holes punched in it so that the baby gibbon could breathe. Claire could hear the baby gibbon shuffling restlessly inside the box, but she did not hear the jingle of the bells attached to his collar. Prachi, Claire guessed, had kept the collar for himself.

"Did you know him?" in bed, Claire asked James. James was getting on top of her.

"Know who?" James stopped.

"The pilot. The American pilot you said was killed in the plane crash."

"The pilot. Yeah. Of course I knew him. Why are you asking me now?" James rolled off Claire.

"I don't know. I just am," she said.

"For chrissakes, Claire, you must admit you have a pretty weird sense of timing. His name, if you must know, is David. David Medina. He's from Pittsburgh. Pittsburgh, Pennsylvania, and he has—or I should say, he had—a wife and two kids. A boy and a girl. Are you satisfied now?"

In the heavy teak bed, James turned away from Claire.

11

At the banquet in the Shangri-La Restaurant, Claire wore a sleeveless linen dress. Dr. Ammundsen was right, the bite healed quickly—after five days Claire could barely find the spot just above the elbow where the baby gibbon had bitten her—but the stains on the new red silk dress, despite Noi's strenuous efforts to wash them, did not come out. The new red silk dress was ruined.

Except for James, Claire was the only westerner at the table. She sat in a row of women who wore low-cut dresses and piled-up hairdos and sipped Fantas—the sweet orange drink—through bright red lips.

"*Kun poot par sar ang grit dai mai?*"—Do you speak English?

Claire turned to speak to the woman next to her and the woman giggled:

"*Di chan poot sar ang grit dai nit noi*"—I don't speak much English.

Across the table from the women, sitting in another row, the men drank Johnny Walker Scotch whiskey. Instead of their uniforms, they wore sport shirts. Opposite Claire,

Captain Ruengrit was wearing a loose Hawaiian shirt with a print of a dancing woman in a hula-skirt. James, his hair freshly combed down with water, was sitting next to Captain Ruengrit.

Gairng som plar chorn! tom kloeng! neua patnam man hoy! When the waiters came in, they shouted out the names of each new steaming dish: *moo sa! pat peht plar duk! gai pat king! hor mok plar! peht yarng!* And as each dish was brought in, one of Captain Ruengrit's fellow officers in the Queen Cobra Regiment stood up, raised his whiskey glass, made a toast. When the toast was finished, the men drained their glasses and banged the glasses down on the table. Right away, too, the glasses were refilled to the brim with more Scotch whiskey. Once a glass broke and across the table a woman in a pink dress let out a little shriek.

The more the men drank, the more they became red-faced and unsteady on their feet, the more their speeches became garbled. At the far end of the table a man on crutches stood up.

Boom! Bavroom!

Instead of making a toast to the new dish, he made noises—the noise of bombs dropping, the noise of bombs hitting their targets, bombs exploding:

Boom! Bavroom!

When James stood up, he looked twice as tall, twice as big. His short-sleeved light blue sport shirt was covered with dark patches of sweat. *Sunak mahk mahk krap*—James did an imitation of the dancing woman in the hula-skirt on Captain Ruengrit's shirt—*mahk*—James bumped his hips one way—*mahk*—he bumped his hips the other way. The men clapped their hands, stamped their feet, hooted and laughed; the women giggled.

Next Captain Ruengrit struggled to his feet. Still laughing, he staggered, lost his balance. Too late James reached out to him. To save himself and no longer laughing, Captain Ruengrit grabbed the tablecloth. Knocking over his chair but hanging on to the tablecloth, Captain Ruengrit fell backward. The dishes, the food, the glasses, the bottles of Johnny Walker Scotch, the bottles of Fanta, everything on the table crashed to the floor.

Quickly, everyone stood up. The women made little cluck-clucking noises as they stepped away from the table. The waiters came running up. Frowning, the manager of the Shangri-La hurried over; he was holding a pad and pencil in his hand.

More plates and glasses broke as Captain Ruengrit tried to get back on his feet. James leaned over to help him, but the captain had reached inside his Hawaiian sport shirt with the dancing woman in the hula-skirt, and pulled out a gun— a .38 caliber police service pistol.

First Captain Ruengrit pointed the pistol at James. Then, slowly, deliberately, he turned and pointed the pistol at the man on his other side. He pointed—this time it looked more like a casual wave—the pistol across the now bare banquet table at the row of women in their low-cut dresses. Next he pointed the pistol at the manager of the Shangri-La who was still holding the pad and pencil but was standing frozen in his tracks. The only sound Claire heard, beside the beating of her heart, was the sound of a glass rolling under the table. Someone started to hiccough, and slowly, slowly, like in a game she had played as a child where the object was to move in without being seen, only this time she had to move away, Claire started to back up from the table.

When James and Claire met again in the parking lot of the Shangri-La Restaurant, they heard three shots. Then silence before a woman began to scream. The woman screamed and screamed as James put the key in the ignition and started up the noisy engine of the Land Rover.

"The weird thing about that Dakota plane crash," James said on the way home in the Land Rover, "was that the cow survived."

"Cow? What cow?" Claire asked.

"The cow that was part of the cargo. They were going to drop the cow to some Laotian troops."

"A live cow? You mean they throw a live cow out of the plane?"

"They do it all the time. They fly as low as they can. The cow is going to be slaughtered anyway."

"The poor cow," Claire said.

"We found the cow not far from the runway, not far from the burning wreckage of the plane with the three guys trapped inside it. The cow was munching away on grass like nothing had happened."

Cow cow cow cow cow—

"Here's another one." In the British Library on Suriwongse Road, the librarian from Melbourne, Australia, was saving the newspaper articles for Claire. "None of it makes any sense. A bloody mystery, if you ask me."

Mr. Thompson and Mrs. Connie Mangskau, an old friend, set off from Penang for the Cameron Highlands on March 23rd in a taxi, Claire read. *The taxi halted at a ferry. A man appeared and spoke to the driver. The driver stepped out of the taxi, making way for the newcomer. He explained that he was the original driver's brother and that the driver "has something to do today, so I will drive you." The taxi drove on to Tappa, a road junction at the foot of the hills leading to the Highlands. Mrs. Mangskau noticed a red warning light on the dashboard. The driver said the car was overheated and drove it into a garage. After inspection he said that he could not possibly drive the car up the hills and suggested that Mr. Thompson and Mrs. Mangskau use a taxi parked nearby. Two men were sitting in the other taxi in addition to the driver. After some discussion—heated on Mrs. Mangskau's part—the two men got out and the visitors continued their trip to the Highlands. Neither Mr. Thompson nor Mrs. Mangskau thought much of the incident at the time.*

"You're right," Claire told the librarian. "It doesn't make any sense."

"This time, love, if you could get us some menthol cigarettes. I told my husband if he doesn't bloody well quit smoking soon, he's going to end up in hospital with bronchitis."

On the Sunday afternoon that Mr. Thompson disappeared, a worker at the garage at Tappa noticed five cars bearing Thai license plates going up the road to the Highlands at about 3:30 P.M. They were a black Chevrolet, a Cortina with a white top and a maroon body, two Volkswagens and a Volkswagen bus. At 5:30 P.M., after Mr. Thompson was last seen at the bungalow, the five cars returned down the mountain road. Claire finished reading the article.

The antique store was situated in the lobby of the Erawan Hotel—the same hotel the woman who was shot during the attempted coup had worked in. Each time Claire had gone before, the store had been shut. Now, although the store was open, she hesitated. Next door was a travel agency. Claire looked at a poster showing a blond woman in a bikini scuba-diving off the Grand Barrier Reef; she studied the discount fares to Bali, Java, and Borneo. When, finally, she opened the door to the antique store, a little bell rang.

"May I help you?" from the back someone asked in polite, precise English.

"No—yes," Claire stuttered. "I mean, I'm just looking."

"You're welcome to look around." A slender, tidy-looking Chinese woman in her fifties came forward. She was polite still.

Claire moved carefully among the lacquer tables, the painted chests, the stone and wooden statues of gods and goddesses, the stacked china bowls. She picked up a blue and white bowl similar to one she had bought at Nakorn Kasem, the Thieves Market—this one looked older, more valuable.

"Lovely, isn't it? Ming dynasty." The woman was looking at Claire expectantly.

"Are you Connie Mangskau—Mrs. Mangskau? Jim Thompson's friend?" Claire asked, introducing herself.

"Did you know Jimmy?" Connie Mangskau frowned. "Or are you another one of those reporters?"

"No, I'm not a reporter, but I did meet Mr. Thompson. My husband and I had dinner—" Claire started to say.

"Thank God. I've talked to so many reporters I've lost count. I had to shut my store on account of the reporters. They asked me so many questions."

"We had dinner with him a few days before he disappeared. I've never seen such a beautiful house, such beautiful art."

"Jimmy was enraptured by Bangkok." Connie Mangskau sighed. "From the first day he got here, it was as if Jimmy had finally arrived somewhere he had belonged all along."

"I read how you went to the Cameron Highlands with Mr. Thompson and how you had to change taxis," Claire said.

"That's typical of what happens in this part of the world," Connie Mangskau answered. "At the time, it didn't strike us as very important—only inconvenient."

"I know. Every time I take a samlor, the driver wants to stop first and buy a bowl of noodles."

"Actually, Jimmy and I joked about it. We knew that the second driver was not really the first driver's brother, the way he told us. We even speculated on what the first driver had to go do. Jimmy suggested that he had to go take his driver's test. As for the second taxi, the taxi in Tappa with the man and the woman in it—"

"Oh, I thought the newspaper said there were two men in the taxi."

Connie Mangskau shook her tidy head. "A man and a woman. The woman, I remember, had her arm in a sling. Jimmy was perfectly willing to share the taxi with them—he felt sorry for the woman with her arm in a sling—but since we had already paid the driver for our own taxi, to drive further with two strangers seemed unnecessary to me."

"I see," Claire said. She did—she saw a fleet of taxis: *saam*, no, more, *see, ha, hok, jet* taxis. "I am sure you did the right thing." Claire picked up the blue and white Ming bowl again. She turned the bowl around in her hands. "Do you think changing taxis had something to do with Mr. Thompson's disappearance?"

"I don't know what to think anymore. All of a sudden it seems as if each event, no matter how mundane or trivial, has taken on significance." Connie Mangskau spoke slowly, she chose her words carefully. "If, for example, on our way up to the Highlands, we had run over a dog—one of those mangy, emaciated dogs one sees along the road—wouldn't that have also been perceived as a sign? Or if after you leave my store," Connie Mangskau was smiling at Claire now, "you go out and murder someone, and the police come around to question me, I would try hard to remember something in your behavior that would provide them with a clue. 'Oh, yes, indeed,' I might say to the police, 'I saw her pick up a very rare and expensive blue and white Ming bowl and I was afraid she was going to drop it, she seemed so distracted.'"

"It's a beautiful bowl," Claire said, putting the bowl down.

The bell attached to the door rang then, and two people walked in—tourists. The man held a camera, maps, guidebooks, the woman had her arm in a sling; Connie Mangskau greeted them in German.

"If you decide you want to buy the Ming bowl," Connie Mangskau called out after Claire as she was leaving the store, "I'll make you a good price for it."

12

THE ROAD FROM BANGKOK TO PATTAYA WAS ROUGH AND full of potholes; the day was exceedingly hot, humid. All of a sudden it began to rain. The rain came down so hard and fast that the windshield wipers of the Land Rover got stuck. James had to work them back and forth by hand.

"Shit," James said.

Claire was practicing her Thai out loud. "*Yee-sip-et, yee-sip-sawng, yee-sip-saam, yee-sip-see, yee-sip-ha.*"

"Can you quit that," James said.

"I told you, didn't I, how I met Connie Mangskau? I talked to her about Jim."

"Jim who?"

"Jim Thompson, of course. Connie Mangskau is an old friend of his. She was with him. They were visiting some people called Ling," Claire said.

"Ling, I know—a Chinese name." James was still working the windshield wipers by hand.

"They're antique dealers," Claire continued. "I read in the paper how the Lings own a chain of antique stores in Singapore, in Hong Kong, all over Southeast Asia." She peered through the windshield, barely able to make out the road. "Connie Mangskau owns the antique store in the Erawan Hotel."

"Is she Chinese, too?"

"Half Chinese. She has beautiful things."

James put his hand on the horn, kept it there. Out the side window, Claire caught a glimpse of a woman swerving on a bicycle.

"Jesus, did you see that woman! She's going to get herself killed. What was I saying? Oh, yeah. You have to be careful, Claire. You can't trust the Chinese."

"How do you mean—*trust?*" Claire turned to look at James, but James kept his eyes fixed on the road. "What about Siri? Siri is half Chinese, isn't he?"

"Siri is different. Claire, I can't see a goddamn thing."

"*Yee-sip-hok, yee-sip-jet, yee-sip-pat, yee-sip-gao, saam-sip,*" Claire continued, under her breath, to count to herself.

"*Tao rai*—how much you pay for your skirt, Claire?" Siri's wife, Priya, right away wanted to know. Priya was as lovely as Claire had imagined—slender, graceful, with long dark hair—but she was not, as Claire had also imagined, waiting to run away from Siri with her childhood sweetheart. Priya was more preoccupied with how she looked, with what she wore, her jewelry, her clothes; with Claire's.

"*Tao rai* you pay for your sandals, Claire?" Priya could hardly wait to ask her next. "Oh, too much!" "*Tao rai* you pay for your gold wedding ring, Claire?" Joyfully clapping her hands together, Priya had to know. "Oh, much too much!"

James and Claire were spending the weekend with Siri and Priya at the beach. The beach was crowded with American and Thai families, their children; it was crowded with soldiers on leave from the nearby port, Sattahip. The soldiers were sunburnt, noisy, they drank beer, most of them had women with them. Instead of a woman, one soldier had a honey bear on a leash. The honey bear looked hot, listless, sick.

Although Claire liked to swim, she liked to swim in a pool, a pool that was clean. In Pattaya she worried about sharks. The Bay of Siam, she had read, was their breeding ground. She did not dare swim her usual crawl, nor did she dare swim very far, no further than where she could still touch bottom with her feet. Also, she kept her head out of the water; that way she could look out for sharks' fins. From time to time Claire looked back at James on the beach.

James had his arms around Priya's slender waist. James had worked one summer as a counselor at a girls' camp and he offered to teach Priya how to swim in the sea. Priya was wearing a perfect-fitting white Lycra bathing suit; she did not want to get her hair wet. Each time a small wave came, Priya struggled out of James's arms to stand up. Priya was laughing—so was James laughing—and although Claire would never swear she actually saw this—the heat distorted things, or Claire imagined it—to her, from where she was swimming, it looked as if every time Priya raised her head out of the water, James bent his to kiss her on the lips.

Siri never once left the beach bungalow. Siri said he was allergic to the sun; he said the one thing he liked to do when he was on vacation in Pattaya was to cook. A long white apron tied around his large stomach, Siri had stayed in the kitchen all day, cleaning, cutting, chopping food. He was preparing something special, he told James, as he wiped the sweat off his large forehead, dishes his mother used to cook for him: *a led snapper steamed in coconut husks, remon shlimp soup, sleet and soul chicken, Chinese flied cabbage,* and you betcha, *lice.*

During dinner that evening, James sucked noisily on the fish bones to show Siri how much he was enjoying the meal. James also went on to tell Siri how much he liked the food in Thailand, and how he could eat anything no matter how spicy or hot: duck eggs soaked in horses' urine, rooster testicles, cobra; in Nakhon Phanom he had eaten dog meat—a German shepherd who got run over by a jeep. And Siri told James that he bet he could offer James at least one dish he would refuse to eat.

Immediately James shot out his hand across the table and said, "You're on, Siri. How much?"

"Ten thousand *baht*," Siri answered.

"Ten thousand *baht*? You didn't really eat a German shepherd, did you, James? You were kidding," Claire said.

Siri raised his glass of rice wine in a toast to James. "To America, to our friend."

"The meat was really tough, stringy." James winked at Claire, then he raised his glass, drained the rice wine. "To Thailand."

"That's disgusting. I don't believe you."

"Thailand is a free country, free from communism." Siri had started up his refrain.

"Thailand is turning into a giant aircraft carrier."

"What did you say, Claire? Thailand is turning into a what?" James lowered his glass, frowned at her.

"I said Thailand is turning into a giant aircraft carrier," Claire repeated.

"Where did you hear that crap?"

Ignoring James, Claire turned and asked Priya, "Did you enjoy learning how to swim with James? Is James a good teacher?"

"James is number one teacher. With James I am not afraid. James is strong man." Priya giggled. "James says he can teach me how to swim just like you, Claire."

"That's good," Claire said, avoiding James. "Thanks, no more fish for me, Siri. It's delicious."

"Every afternoon, I play mah-jongg with my friends in Bangkok. I can teach you, Claire," Priya also volunteered.

Later in bed, inside the breezy wooden bungalow, Claire turned her back on James. When James tried to pull her toward him, she shrugged off his hand.

"What's wrong?" he asked. "I was just kidding about eating the dog. The German shepherd."

"Nothing. My stomach."

"What's wrong with your stomach? Do you feel sick?"

"The fish," Claire answered. "Siri's fish did not agree with me."

As always it took Claire a long time to fall asleep. She lay awake listening to James snore lightly and to the waves pound against the beach. The waves, she imagined, were full of sharks.

Early the next morning, before Siri and Priya were up, James and Claire went for a run on the beach. On their way back, they walked hand-in-hand and splashed the blue warm water into spray with their feet. Claire was looking down for shells.

"Come on. Let's go." James pulled hard at her hand.

"What?" Claire looked up.

A few yards from them on the beach, a man was on top of a woman. His naked white butt pumped up and down as he grunted. The woman was on her hands and knees, her long dark hair was sweeping back and forth in the sand with the pumping motion; she was throwing up. Next to her another man was getting to his feet, he was pulling up his pants. When he saw James and Claire walk by looking, he grinned and put his hand to his forehead in a gesture of mock salute.

"Come on." James pulled harder at Claire's hand.

After they had gone past, Claire asked, "What about the woman?"

James did not answer.

"The Lust-Thanat Communique," Claire said under her breath.

Back in Bangkok, James and Claire had their first fight. The fight started because James was late. He came home after midnight, long after dinner was served. The dinner got cold. Claire ate a small portion of the cold dinner before Lamum took it away. First Claire telephoned, but no one answered at the JUSMAAG headquarters; the switchboard was shut. Next she questioned Prachi: *Nai* James had not told Prachi that he would be home late? *Nai* James had not said he had to go up to Nakhon Phanom again? Each time, sure, Prachi shook his head. Claire resisted the temptation to call Siri—what would she say? Instead she sat in the living room trying to read, but mainly she waited—her ears straining for the sound of the Land Rover, her eyes straying from the pages of her book toward the garden gate.

King Vajiravudh decreed that all Siamese should adopt a surname. This new law intended to weed out Chinese surnames also created a great deal of confusion . . . Claire had read this part already. She turned to the next chapter: *King Prajadhipok dropped the gold standard that linked the Thai baht to the pound sterling, but this measure came too late to stem the tide of the worldwide economic crisis of* . . .

It could, Claire imagined, have started innocently enough with James calling Siri and Priya answering the phone. James and Priya talked for a few minutes; they joked about continuing the swimming lessons. James might even have invited Priya over to the house—one day soon, prefer-ably on the weekend—and he would teach her in the pool.

A swimming pool, Claire could hear James explain to convince Priya, was an easier place to learn how to swim than the sea . . .

James said he had been at a meeting.

"You're lying! I telephoned. No one was there," Claire shouted at him when he finally walked in the door.

The meeting, James said, had gone on longer than he had anticipated.

"You could have called!"

James started to say something else, but Claire would not let him. "I don't want to hear your lies!"

"Lies? Claire, what are you talking about?"

"You were out—out at some nightclub, I bet, with—" Claire picked something off the coffee table—a bowl. The blue and white bowl she had bought at Nakorn Kasem was wide of the mark. The fragile china splintered when it hit the floor.

"I'm sick of it here," she yelled. "I want to leave!"

Claire tried to pick up something else—her glass. James grabbed her wrist. He was angry now.

"If you leave," he shouted at her, "don't bother to come back!"

That night they slept in separate rooms. In the spare bedroom Claire hardly closed her eyes. She lay facing the door waiting for James to come in. He would make love to her; afterward he would assume everything was all right. But James never came in. He left early the next morning. Claire heard the noisy Land Rover start up.

After James left, Claire tried to piece the blue and white bowl back together. The fragments were too small; some of them were dust. She sniffed back tears. When Noi asked her if she wanted something to eat, Claire shook her head. She went back to bed—their bed. She lay down on James's side, it was still warm. She put her face into his pillow, she could smell him. James smelled of ironed shirts.

In Claire's dream King Vajiravudh decreed that after the next eclipse of the sun all foreigners had to change their names to *rapprathaan* . . .

Siri telephoned later the same day.

"Tell James to go to the bank," Siri told Claire.

"The bank? Which bank?" She had forgotten about James and Siri's bet.

"How's your wife, Priya?" Claire also said. "Tell her to come and swim in our pool."

James lost his bet, and Siri, no doubt, just broke even. The cost of the monkey, the special table with the hole in the middle, the electric saw, finding a place for the meal, bribing people, James said, must have added up to at least ten thousand *baht*. The whole thing was highly illegal.

"What kind of monkey brains?" Claire could not resist asking him. "A baby gibbon's?"

13

Every afternoon during the month of May, it rained with such suddenness and force that if Claire was in the garden spraying the rose bushes or picking hibiscus blooms, in just a few seconds, the time it took her to run back to the house, her hair, her clothes were soaked through. In those few seconds, the rain fell so hard and fast that it obliterated everything from view—the garden gate on one side of the house and, on the other, the canal. The noise, too, of the rain drowned out all sounds—the sound even of Noi's baby boy crying at the sight of her.

"Noi!" Claire called as she ran upstairs to the bedroom to change her wet clothes.

"Prachi!" She yelled for him to close the wooden shutters to the house.

Neither Noi nor Prachi could hear Claire as the rain fell through the open doors and spattered on the living room floor and on the new grass rug. The rain streamed through the flimsy window screens and splashed on the new sofa slip-cover, the new sofa cushions. Soon, too, the dampness would cause mildew to grow on the newly painted white walls.

"Noi! Prachi!" she screamed.

Afterward, the sky, as if suddenly transfused with blue, was clear. It was less humid, too. For a brief time the weather in Bangkok was like that of an ordinary hot summer day on Cape Cod. For once the seasons nearly coincided.

In June every summer, as long as Claire could remember and ever since she was a child, she and her parents went to the same house. The house was situated on a bluff, and even during the worst of the heat, there was always a cool breeze from the sea. And each summer, too, as long as Claire could remember, her parents' routine never varied. In the morning Claire's mother gardened while Claire's father wrote or read; in the afternoon they played tennis. Claire could picture how worn her father's sneakers looked on the tennis court, how he and her mother both claimed to prefer their old wood rackets. Later her parents went down to the beach to swim. Before dinner they sat outside on the lawn and had a drink— her mother always drank vodka, her father gin. From where they sat, her parents heard the pounding of the sea, they smelled the neighbor's barbecue.

Up to a certain point Claire could picture them exactly— how her mother was dressed in her denim wraparound skirt, a vertical rose thorn scratch on one of her brown legs, how her father was wearing khakis and was puffing on his pipe. Claire could smell the smoke, the odor of the pipe tobacco mingling with that of the barbecue. Then, almost imperceptibly in front of her eyes, her parents' orderly lives began to change. Claire could still picture her mother driving the old Saab to the village to buy groceries—but had her mother's hair turned gray all of a sudden? And why, Claire wondered, was her mother driving at night? Claire's father was with her in the car. He was wearing a sweater—the sweater was a garish red, a color her father would never wear. In addition

Claire's mother and father were arguing: *All you ever think about is your damn academic career. You never think about me!* Claire's mother's voice was shrill, she sounded close to tears; Claire's father's voice, when he answered her, was angry, harsh: *You always act like a spoilt child, you always act—* Claire did not want to hear any more.

There were too many variables all of a sudden. Too much could happen in a single day. A delivery van—a white one and thus harder to see—could run the single stop sign in the village and plow right into her parents' old Saab. The slower car always bore the brunt of the accident; the driver of the van would not be hurt. *Oh, my God!* he would cry. *I didn't see the sign!*

For her parents, Claire realized, it was not yet today, it was still yesterday. They were a day behind. If today was Tuesday, for them it was still Monday. The idea was as chilling, to Claire, as news of their death.

"*Mem? Mem?*" Noi was climbing the stairs two at a time. Had Claire called her?

Wani—today.
   Phrang ni—tomorrow.
   Miss Pat recited the days of the week for Claire:
   wan athit
   wan janwan
   wan angkaan
   wan put
   wan paruhat
   wan suk
   wan saw

For the kitchen Claire bought an aluminum box. She set the box on top of the charcoal pit and baked a *gai* in it. To brown the *gai* she heaped burning charcoal on top of the aluminum box. Lamum and Noi watched Claire. They always fried food, it was quicker. While Claire was basting the *gai*, she counted out loud for them in English.

Lamum and Noi giggled—*wan tu srii fo.*

Wan, tu, srii, fo—

Claire was giving Lamum and Noi English lessons. The baby boy with the silver net over his penis was napping, and Prachi was fishing the bougainvillea leaves out of the swimming pool with the long net the way he always did. Prachi already knew how to speak English, he said. But by the third day, Prachi left his net and joined Lamum and Noi on the terrace. So did the woman who bathed in the canal every morning without exposing any bare flesh. Since he had no passengers, the taxi boatman tied up his boat at their landing; so did the coffee vendor; so did the boatman who sharpened the knives.

Fo, fie, see, thaivin, ait.

Claire had to enunciate; she had to make her voice accentless; she had to speak as clearly and distinctly as possible—like the English schoolteacher Anna Leonowens, whose book Claire had read and seen performed as a musical play.

"Five, six, seven, eight, nine," Claire repeated for them.

The terrace might be transformed into a stage and Claire imagined herself up on that stage, snapping her fingers, stamping her feet, twirling her skirt for Lamum, Noi, for Prachi, for the woman who bathed in the canal, the taxi boatman, the coffee vendor, the man who sharpened the knives. It made no difference that she could hardly carry a tune, that she could never remember the lyrics to a song; she would make them up as she went along. Lamum, Noi, Prachi, the others would not know the difference or notice if she sang off-key: *Shall we dance? Tum, tum, tum. Shall we dance? On a bright cloud of music shall we fly? Tum, tum, tum. Shall we still be together with our arms around each other, shall we dance? Shall we dance?* In the musical play, Anna and King Mongkut, a mismatched but oddly moving pair, had waltzed, and Claire would begin with Noi—the prettiest, the most graceful. She would lead: *wan, tu, srii.* Claire would waltz with Lamum. Then with Prachi, even if she was taller than he: *wan, tu, srii.* Claire would put her hand on Prachi's bare back; she would get to feel the muscles James did not have: *wan, tu, srii, wan, tu, srii.*

Getting to know you, getting to know all about you— Claire was humming to herself when James came back from Nakhon Phanom. "Guess what?" she said.

"*Happy Talk, keep talkin' Happy Talk! Talk about things you'd like to do. You gotta have a dream*—" James answered, mimicking the high-pitched voice of a woman singing.

"That's from *South Pacific.* A different show. I'm teaching Lamum, Noi, Prachi, everyone how to count."

"Count what?"

"Count in English—one, two, three."

"Ditto—I'm teaching the Laotians how to count the trucks on the Ho Chi Minh Trail." Again mimicking a woman singer's high-pitched voice, James named the sensors he was testing. "Seismic, acoustic, antimagnetic."

"James, I'm serious!"

"Yeah, I'm serious, too. Dead serious."

"Five, six, seven, eight."

"You should go out more," James told Claire then. "Make some friends."

Nine, ten, eleven, twelve—Claire continued in her head.

What if she reached a million? A million and thirteen, a million and fourteen, a million and fifteen?

In Nakorn Kasem, the Thieves Market, Claire was learning to bargain; she was learning to recognize the different periods of Thai art: Khmer, Dvaravati, Sukothai, U–Thong, Lopburi; she could tell apart the statues of the Buddhas; the Bodhisattvas; Vishnu; Uma and Siva on top of their bull, Nandi; Hari-Hara holding a seashell in one hand, a disk in the other; the smiling stone head of the sun god, Suriya; the half-male, half-female figure of the deity, Ardhanari; Prajnaparamita, the goddess of wisdom; and the destroyer of ignorance, Chanda-li.

She liked to examine the fragile Bencharong bowls; she liked to study the intricacy of their designs, the perfectly rendered details, the flower petals, the arabesque of leaves, garlands, the edges trimmed in gold leaf, the fluted rims, the crosshatched geometric patterns that separated a lip from a lid, a lotus blossom in full bloom, next to it a little bud. Sometimes the owner of the store offered Claire a tiny cup of bitter Chinese green tea; the cup was so fragile that if Claire held the it too tightly the cup might snap.

From Nakorn Kasem she walked down narrow Soi Wanit to Pahurat, then on to Chareon Krung Road which turned into New Road, past Wat Timitr, past the French and Portuguese embassies, past Bangrak Market with the mounds of fruit, the piles of vegetables, the bunches of sweet-smelling flowers, until Claire reached Suriwongse Road and the Thai Silk Company.

Opening the door to the store, she said, "I am just looking."

Claire was looking for the woman with the French accent, the woman who had sold her the silk—Mrs. Perera. But Mrs. Perera, Claire was told, had left. Mrs. Perera's hus-

band had been transferred to another newspaper in Kuala
Lumpur.

"I'm looking for silk for my mother," she said, changing
her mind.

The bolts of shiny silks were arranged on the shelves
according to color: *see narm ngerm*—blue, *see keaw*—green,
see dairng—red, *see leuang*—yellow.

"Your mother? What does your mother look like? Does
your mother look like you?" the salesperson wanted to know.

"Yes. No. Her hair is gray now," Claire replied.

"Lightweight silk for a dress?"

Down came a bolt. Next came a darker one. Four beige
silk bolts. And navy, French blue, indigo, azure, aquamarine,
turquoise silks. Or did she prefer green? A plaid? More bolts
of multicolored silk came tumbling down and were spread
out on the teak floor.

"What sort of a dress? An evening dress?"

Heavier, richer silks. Silks with gold and silver threads.

"A two-piece suit? An evening coat?"

Printed silks with chrysanthemums, lotus flowers, birds
of paradise, cockatoos—in bright greens, vivid oranges, pur-
ples and pinks.

"A skirt? A blouse? A scarf?" The salesperson was tiring.

See dairng orn—light red.

See dairng kehm—dark red.

What was today? *Wan athit? wan janwan? wan angkaan?
wan put?* Her mother, Claire worried, might already be dead.

Lead.

14

In ADDITION TO THE CHINA SAUCEBOAT WHICH HAD belonged to her grandmother, Claire's gold pin was missing. The gold pin was in the shape of an artist's palette and had little precious stones set in it—the stones stood for the different colored paints. The gold pin, Claire swore to James, had been inside a leather jewelry box in her top bureau drawer, along with her scarves, her underwear—Claire did not mention the photograph of Jim Thompson—which were all still there.

"You're sure you didn't wear it? You're sure you didn't lose it somewhere?" James asked her.

"I'm positive. The pin was right here."

"No one's touched this." James took the Smith & Wesson .44 magnum out of his bureau drawer. Spinning open the cylinder, James unloaded the gun and held out the bullets, before he reloaded it, clicked shut the cylinder, and put the gun back in the drawer. "If someone wanted to steal something, they'd steal this—not a pin."

"A gold pin. A pin with little emeralds, little rubies and sapphires."

"Don't worry, Claire, the pin will turn up somewhere," James said.

"You think Noi stole it? Noi or Prachi?"

James shook his head. "Prachi is lazy, but Prachi, I'm sure, would not steal."

Pai nai ka?—where are you going?

Sa tah nee rot meh—the bus station.

Sa tah nee rot fai—the railway station.

Sa tah nee tam ruat—the police station, Miss Pat said.

But never, never, under any circumstances should Claire go to the police, was another of the things James warned her about, along with telling her how he would sleep better when he was away in Nakhon Phanom if he knew a man like Prachi was in the house. And should Claire have an accident, should Claire get into any kind of trouble, James went on to say, Claire should go directly to the American Embassy.

"What is the Thai word for embassy?" Claire asked Miss Pat.

Sa tahn thut.

At the American Embassy, Claire waited at the gate while a marine guard examined her passport. "Your passport expires in three months," the guard told her drily as he handed it back to her. "I know. Why I'm here," Claire answered him.

A jeep driven by a soldier stopped at the embassy gate; the marine guard saluted, waved the soldier-driven jeep in. A man in uniform got out of the jeep. Politely the man in uniform waved Claire in first through the embassy door.

"Thank you."

"You're welcome," he answered at the same time as someone called out to him: "Good to see you, General Black. Right this way, General Black. Ambassador Martin is expecting you."

Too late Claire said, "Oh, General Black." In his uniform she had not recognized him. She watched as General Black was escorted through a door with a sign: OFFICE OF THE AMBASSADOR.

After getting the forms she needed for a new passport— she would also need new passport photos—and before leaving the embassy, Claire paused a moment in the reception area. The embassy was air-conditioned; outside it was nearly a hundred humid degrees. On a table there was a stack of American magazines: *Time, Newsweek, Life.* An old copy of *The New York Times* was lying on top of the magazines. Claire began to read:

TAYNINH, South Vietnam—At 9:20 last night, an evacuation helicopter touched down on a field lit by flares. Four medics slid a stretcher out and ran 100 feet to the admitting ward of the 45th Surgical Hospital near here.

The barely conscious man on the stretcher was 19 years old, a rifleman in the First Infantry Divison. He was one of 25,000 men taking part in Operation Junction City, the major United States offensive near Cambodia.

One bullet had caught him in the shoulder, and a second had left a gaping hole in his chest.

The stretcher was placed on an examining table and three Army physicians, three nurses and three enlisted men went to work.

"Can you take a deep breath for me?" Captain John F. Stahler probed the entry wound in the soldier's chest.

The chest began to heave. ". . . Oh, oh, oh. Please, doctor."

"Easy, friend," said Dr. Stahler. "Easy now. Easy does it."

He turned away and with surgical scissors began notching holes on one end of a rubber tube. "He's hurt bad," the doctor said. "Lung is full of blood and there's no telling how much other damage has been done, but there's a lot."

The operation began at 10 P.M. and the doctors found that the bullet had passed through the right lung, pierced the diaphragm, torn away a section of the colon, shattered the spleen and badly damaged the liver and the right kidney.

The surgeons faced an enormously difficult task that could only be attempted on a young patient with a strong heart. The spleen and the right kidney were removed and the delicate job of repairing the liver was begun.

At midnight one of the nurses stepped outside for a cigarette. "He's a tough boy," she said.

At 1 a.m. the surgical team was still bent over the operating table. The internal bleeding could not be stopped: the pile of empty blood bags grew higher. By the time the operation was over, the soldier had received 28 pints.

At 2:15, the major work was completed and the surgeons turned to the pierced lung. But at 2:30, suddenly, the heartbeat got weaker and finally stopped.

Claire looked up. General Black was leaving the office of the ambassador. He was picking up his cap. Putting down *The New York Times*, Claire called out to him.

"Oh, general. General Black!"

Ambassador Martin's aide had General Black by the arm and was talking to him as he escorted him to the door. General Black glanced up.

"I met you—" Claire started to say. "We met at Jim Thompson's house."

"That's right," General Black nodded politely. "Good to see you again, young lady." He turned back to Ambassador Martin's aide.

"There's no news is there—I mean about Jim Thompson?" Claire was running after him. "I heard the search for him has been called off."

"The official search, but there's a psychic up there now—

the one who helped solve the Boston Strangler case—Hurkos, Peter Hurkos. He's in the Highlands with his assistant, a blond woman. She said she was some kind of a movie star." General Black shook his head and turned again to Ambassador Martin's aide. "To me, she didn't look as if she could act her way out of a paper bag."

Ambassador Martin's aide said something that Claire only half heard. General Black nodded. "You're right. The money, too, is attracting all kinds of crazy people. I spoke to a local witch doctor, a *bomoh*, who swore to me that Jim was trapped inside a big banyan tree. We looked in the banyan tree and found nothing." General Black adjusted his cap more firmly on his head. "So what were you saying, Ben, about General Thanom's statement to the press?"

"But you think Jim Thompson was kidnapped?" again too late Claire called after him.

She watched as General Black walked out the embassy door, his stride quick and full of purpose. Even from the back General Black looked like someone who was capable—more than capable, Claire imagined—of finding a man lost in the jungle.

And what had he said that Claire read? *A body is different. A body should not be hard to find in the jungle. Vultures fly over it. Animals are attracted . . .*

At ten o'clock every Thursday morning the snakes at the Pasteur Institute were milked of their venom. The venom, the guide explained, was used for serum. Three large pits were filled with king cobras, cobras, banded kraits, vipers—about a dozen snakes lay inside each pit. The snakes' thick mottled bodies were twined around each other; some of the snakes were more than ten feet long.

"Snakes are not naturally aggressive. Snakes only attack

if provoked," the guide was telling the group of JUSMAAG officers' wives.

The JUSMAAG officer's wife named Deirdre said, "*Raht.*"

Inside the first pit a man in a dirty white jacket—the kind of jacket an orderly or a doctor might wear—had picked up a king cobra and was holding it by the neck as the big snake slowly disentangled itself from the other snakes in the pit. When the king cobra was dangling free, another man, who was wearing a short-sleeved plaid shirt, inserted a glass plate under the king cobra's fangs. The man in the dirty doctor's jacket squeezed the venom sacks behind the king cobra's eyes and a pale yellowish liquid spurted out onto the glass.

Deirdre said, "Yuk."

When the two men had finished milking all the snakes in the first pit, they took a break. The men went to sit in the shade of a monkeypod tree to eat a bowl of noodles.

Next to Dr. Ammundsen's office on New Road, Claire noticed a photo studio which advertised quick developing. The photographer, a young man, spoke English. He had studied photography in the United States, in Los Angeles. He wanted to be a filmmaker, a movie producer, he told Claire as he got his camera ready, adjusted the chair for her to sit in, unrolled the backdrop. Already he had written a screenplay, an adaption of an old Siamese story: the story of a man and woman from two different hilltribes, Akha and Karen, who fall in love.

"Oh, Akha. I saw an Akha woman in the market—" Claire started to say.

Several people had read the screenplay, liked it, were ready to back the film, the photographer continued, naming people.

Claire shook her head; she had never heard of them. But come to think of it, he asked her, as he ducked his head underneath the black cloth and adjusted the camera lens to focus on her, would Claire do him the great favor of reading the script as well? He had an extra copy in his studio, he would give it to her afterward, but now Claire should open her eyes, hold still, smile and say *cheese*, please.

Noey kairng!

At home Claire asked Prachi to ask Noi if Noi had seen her gold pin. Lamum, Claire knew, rarely left the kitchen.

"*Peen?*" Prachi did not understand. "*Peen?*"

"A gold pin—*torng*." Claire did not know the Thai word for pin. To show Prachi she tried to mime pinning something to her blouse, to her chest right above her breast.

"See, like this. A pin." Looking up she saw Prachi staring at her breast, and Claire all of a sudden blushed. "Ask Noi," she told him instead.

Noi followed Claire upstairs to the bedroom. Claire opened her top bureau drawer, took out the leather jewelry box.

"*Mai mi*—not here. Gold pin." Claire showed Noi.

"*Mai mi*," Noi repeated. "*Gao peun.*"

Gao peun—old friend.

Instead of being away one night a week, the way he was at the beginning, James was often away for two. One week James was away for three nights.

"It's not up to me to decide," James answered when Claire complained. "If it was, believe me, Claire, I wouldn't go near Nakhon Phanom or to any of those godforsaken places."

James dove into the pool.

"Which godforsaken places?"

"Oh, Claire—" In the pool James shook the water out of his ears.

"Godforsaken places where, James?"

"Claire, don't ask me now. Please." James was floating on his back.

If James would not tell her, Claire would find out for herself, she decided. She would look inside James's briefcase, go through his papers; she would look in his wallet, look in his khaki pants and empty out his pockets, his shirt pockets; she would look— No, she would do more than look—she would sniff his dirty socks, his sweaty T–shirt, his stained under-wear, before Noi took them away to be washed, for a clue to where James had been.

"Besides missing me, what did you do this week?" Still on his back, James made a few paddling motions with his hands.

"I saw the snakes being milked at the Pasteur Institute. You should see them, James. A man picks up a cobra, a fifteen-foot king cobra, he squeezes the venom—"

"I thought you went to palaces, to museums. Where is the guide taking you next week? To Dusit Zoo?"

"I don't know, he didn't say. To Hanoi maybe."

"Hanoi? Yeah, right. Over my dead body," James said.

"James, you know what?" Claire asked after a while. She was sitting in the dark watching him.

"Hmm," James answered.

"I asked Prachi and I asked Noi, but I haven't found my gold pin yet."

James kicked a little in the water.

"James," Claire said again.

"Hmm."

"In the paper I read another theory about why Jim Thompson disappeared. He was kidnapped as part of a com-munist plot."

"Bullshit." James gave a bigger kick in the water.

"A communist plot to stop the Americans from flying out of Thailand to bomb Vietnam."

"Bullshit," James said again, louder. "First of all the communists would never choose someone like Thompson. He's too well known, too prominent. When the communists come into a village, they don't kill the village chief or the rich farmer, they kill an innocent bystander—a young boy, an old man who happens to be there. The randomness and the injustice of it has a much stronger psychological effect. It means it could happen to you or to me or to anybody."

When James reached the edge of the pool, he pulled himself out of the water. "Claire? O, *Clair de ma lune*—are you there?"

Claire was upstairs; Claire was looking through James's things.

15

"IF JIM THOMPSON WENT FOR A WALK, THE WAY SOME OF the newspapers I read said," Claire told James the following morning, "he would not have left his cigarettes and his Zippo lighter behind. Jim Thompson was a heavy smoker. During dinner I watched him. He must have smoked at least three or four cigarettes. Thai cigarettes. Another thing, if Jim Thompson was attacked by a wild animal, a leopard or a cobra, the cobra or the leopard would not have swallowed Jim Thompson's sunglasses or Jim Thompson's watch. But if, say," Claire continued, "the cobra or the leopard did, the cobra or leopard would have had to regurgitate or pass something—Jim Thompson's sunglasses, his watch, the zipper on his trousers, the buttons on Jim's—"

"Claire, whoa, do you mind! I'm eating breakfast. Can we talk about something else?" James said.

In 1932, a coup was staged by the leader of the People's Party, Pridi Panomyong. Absolute monarchy was replaced by a dictatorship. In a countercoup, a year later, Pibul Songkhram succeeded in ousting Pridi Panomyong. In 1935, King Prajadhipok had no choice but to abdicate . . .

Too many coups and countercoups, too many unpronounceable names: *Prajadhipok, Pridi Panomyong, Pibul Songkhram.* In the British Library, Claire found it harder and harder to concentrate. Instead she looked through newspapers, leafed through magazines. She read and reread the articles about the missing Jim Thompson so many times she knew them almost by heart:

He was taking some potted plants to friends, I believe, in the Highlands, recalled Bangkok Post Sports Editor Anton Perera, last night. Perera happened to be aboard the same plane as Jim Thompson when Thompson flew out of Don Muang Airport on his way to Penang. He spent the night at the Ambassador Hotel and was leaving the next morning by car for the Highlands, Perera also said.

Claire looked so long and hard at photographs of Jim Thompson that his face became as familiar to her as her father's face, as James's face, as her own face. She swore she would know him anywhere.

"He isn't handsome exactly, but he's a nice looking man," Claire told the librarian from Melbourne, Australia. "Polite, too. I'll never forget the way he took my arm."

"What do I care what he looks like?" The librarian laughed. "He's rich, isn't he? And someone is bound to claim the twenty-five thousand dollars—that's a bloody lot of money. Speaking of money, love, how much do I owe you for the American cigarettes?"

Afterward Claire went back to her books:

During World War II, Pibul Songkhram's government allowed the Japanese in the Gulf of Thailand; Pibul declared war on the United States. Seni Pramoj, the Thai ambassador to Washington, however, refused to deliver the declaration. At the same time a pro-Ally underground resistance movement, the Free Thai Movement, was being formed. The movement received the active support of the former prime minister, Pridi

Panomyong. As the Japanese became increasingly disliked and
as the tide turned against them, Pibul's collaborative govern-
ment collapsed . . . Claire was nearly up to the present day in
her reading.

While a samlor waited for her on New Road, Claire ran into
the studio to pick up her passport photographs. She had not
yet read the photographer's screenplay and she was afraid
he would ask her about it. After paying and thanking him, she
took the envelope of photographs without looking at them.

"These photographs don't even look like me," at home,
Claire told James. "My hair is longer and I look as if I'd
gained ten pounds all of a sudden." She started to laugh. "I
don't even own that kind of a blouse."

"Let's see." James took the photographs from Claire.
"You're right. You have to take them back. The woman isn't
half bad looking—funny, she looks familiar. Who took these
photographs?"

"A Thai. He's a screenwriter actually. He gave me his
screenplay."

"A screenplay about what?"

"I don't know—hilltribes."

In the Thai language, Miss Pat said, there is no gender and
no singular or plural; nouns have a single fixed form. In most
cases the context makes it clear whether a single item or
several items are being referred to; to be specific, a number
can be used with a noun. If, however, a number is used, so
must a classifier, since every noun in the Thai language has
a specific classifier. The classifier for people—except for
monks and royalty—is *kon*; the classifier for cars is *kun*—
Was Claire listening? Miss Pat asked her.

* * *

The next time Claire went to the Erawan Hotel, she went straight to Connie Mangskau's store. Again the little bell rang as she opened the door.

Connie Mangskau looked older, smaller. "Peter Hurkos, the private investigator, was here the other day," she told Claire right away. "He asked me a lot of questions about Jimmy."

"The psychic?" Claire said. "I heard someone mention his name the other day."

"He came with his assistant, a young woman. She was very pretty, blond. As a matter of fact she looked a little like you."

"She's an actress, I think," Claire said.

"I told Peter Hurkos all about how I first met Jimmy when I was working as an interpreter for the Allied Forces. I told him Jimmy was supposed to have parachuted into Thailand—parachuted up north in the jungle—only at the last moment the pilot of the plane got word of the Japanese surrender."

"Parachuted? Good heavens," Claire said.

"From the very first day he got here, Jimmy was enraptured by Bangkok, as if he finally had arrived somewhere he had belonged all along," Connie Mangskau told Claire again.

"Yes, you said—like Thailand was his spiritual home."

"I also told Peter Hurkos about our trip up to the Highlands," Connie Mangskau continued, "and how we had to keep changing taxis and how Jimmy had insisted on getting a haircut."

"A haircut?"

"There is a barbershop in the lobby of the Ambassador Hotel, a barbershop Jimmy said he liked, and I remember saying to him: 'Jimmy, for heaven's sakes, you don't need a haircut now.' This made us late. So late, in fact, that the original taxi could not wait. We had to hire still another taxi."

"I see," Claire said. Again she saw the fleet of taxis: *rot yon saam kun*, no, more, *see, ha, hok, jet kun* taxis. The fleet of taxis was bigger and the taxis were different makes: Chevrolets, Buicks, Volkswagens, Toyotas; and different colors: *see narm ngern, see dam, see keaw, see som, see leuang, see dairng . . .*

"The Ming bowl?" Claire suddenly remembered. "Where's the blue and white Ming bowl?"

"It's gone. I sold the bowl right after you left. To some German tourists," Connie Mangskau answered. "They came in the same day, and I remember thinking, I hope that nice young blond woman doesn't come back for the bowl. Strange, too, how so often I have a piece that no one looks at or has any interest in buying for months, then all of a sudden in a single day, several people want it. I'm sorry."

In the lobby of the Erawan Hotel, across from Connie Mangskau's antique store and across from the travel agency advertising discount fares to Java, Bali, and Borneo and with the poster in the window of a woman in a bikini scuba-diving off the Great Barrier Reef, Claire noticed a beauty parlor. Like Jim Thompson, she, too, decided she needed a haircut.

Afterward Claire stood on the steps of the Erawan Hotel. The sun burned the top of her head; the light hurt her eyes and made her squint. It was so hot the tar in the street was melting. Shoes, sandals that pedestrians had left in their hurry to cross and avoid cars, buses, samlors, were stuck in the tar. The Erawan Hotel was only a few minutes' walk from the American Embassy, but Claire was no longer sure that she would be able to put one foot in front of the other and walk the two or three blocks down Sukhumvit before she had to turn down Wireless Road and walk a few more. She was not sure she would be able to walk through the gate past the marine guard, up the steps and through the reception area. She would not be able to hold the unwieldy, slippery pen in her hand and fill out the passport forms: her birth date, James's birth date, her parents' names which would include her mother's maiden name—*Davison*—their places of birth—*Seattle, Washington; Providence, Rhode Island*—their birth dates.

Taking the passport photos out of her purse, Claire looked at them again. Now with her hair cut, Claire looked more like the woman, and she wondered who the woman was. And what nationality? English? No, the woman was blond and Swedish? Finnish? Did it matter? Would anyone notice the difference?

Dear Will,

I hope you are well and that you will get to go home and go to law school soon. Enclosed is a photo that was supposed to be of me but isn't—

Dear Will,

I hope you are well and I hope you are not in Tayninh. Enclosed is a photo that does not look like me or like Lisa—

Dear Will,

A body is different. A body should not be hard to find in the jungle. Vultures fly over it. Animals are attracted by the smell. Enclosed is—

At home Claire could not write a letter to Will either.

At a cocktail party in honor of Ambassador Ellsworth Bunker—Ambassador Bunker's plane was late, and he had not arrived yet—everyone at the American Embassy, including James and Claire, was glancing expectantly toward the door. On the other side of the crowded room, Claire caught sight of Deirdre, the

JUSMAAG officer's wife, talking to a civilian. Claire waved at her; Deirdre waved back but did not come over.

"Do you think General Black is here?" Claire asked.

"You want a glass of wine?" James answered.

Claire watched as James joined a group of men at the bar. Nearly all the men were in uniform. James nodded or shook hands with most of them. Then James went over and spoke to a Thai. The Thai was also in uniform—an officer, the front of his khaki shirt was covered with decorations. James put his hand on the Thai officer's shoulder; the Thai officer put his hand on James's. The Thai officer said something which made James laugh, and James said something which made the Thai officer laugh.

"Here's your wine." James came back and handed Claire a glass. "I wish you hadn't gone and cut your hair. I liked it better long."

"Cooler," Claire said. "Who was that? The man in the uniform with all the stuff on his chest—the Thai?" She took a sip of her wine.

"Captain Ruengrit. Don't you remember?"

"Oh!" Claire said out loud. She said it the way she might if she had twisted her ankle or if she had missed a step in the dark.

A hush had fallen over the large room.

"Captain Ruengrit is the one who shot somebody in the Shangri-La Restaurant."

"Sshhh—"

Everyone had turned to the door and to the new ambassador.

Claire looked around for Captain Ruengrit. He was shorter than most of the westerners, and in the crowded room Claire could not see him.

"Why is he here?" she whispered to James.

"What do you mean why is he here? He's on his way to Saigon."

"I mean Captain Ruengrit."

"Oh, him." James shrugged his shoulders. "How should I know? Claire, ssshh."

Graham Martin, the ambassador to Thailand, finished introducing Ellsworth Bunker, and Bunker began to speak:

"We look beyond this harsh aggression and cruel conflict to a time of reconciliation and peace throughout Asia. We stand ready to assist the Republic of Vietnam and our other Asian and Pacific friends in building a region of security, order, and progress genuinely founded on Asian traditions and Asian aspirations."

After the applause, James, along with several other men in uniform, raised their hands to ask Ambassador Bunker questions. The ambassador pointed to a man across from where Claire and James were standing—the same man Deirdre had been talking to. Claire could not hear the question; she only heard Ambassador Bunker's reply:

"I'd like to get a picture of what the problem is before commenting on specific problems of the war."

Before James and Claire left the American Embassy, James went up to Ambassador Martin and said a few words to him.

On the way home in the Land Rover, Claire asked James what he had gone up to Ambassador Martin to say, and James answered, "His son was killed in Vietnam. I went to offer him my condolences."

"Oh."

After a while Claire also asked James what he was going to ask Ambassador Bunker anyway, and James replied:

"I was going to ask Ambassador Bunker whether it was okay with him if my wife and the other JUSMAAG officers' wives went to visit Hanoi."

16

For Visakha Puja—the day that celebrates the birth of the Buddha—Claire bought a poinsettia plant. She decorated the plant with tinsel, put it on the dining-room table. In Nakorn Kasem she got James a boar's tusk attached to a gold chain which she told him he could use as a watch fob when, after twenty-five years of dutiful service in the army—if he was lucky—he would be made a general and receive a gold pocket watch, to which James replied that the army, as far as he knew, was not in the habit of making many generals or handing out gold pocket watches, but he was pleased to have the boar's tusk anyway. James bought Claire an embroidered silk scarf. After they had each opened their presents, James said he had to go back up to Nakhon Phanom.

"On Buddha's birthday?" Claire said.

"Don't blame me, Claire. Blame Hanoi. Only believe it or not it's the other way around." James was more talkative than usual. "Hanoi is blaming us for bombing residential areas, harming civilians."

"And are we?"

"Hard to say." James shrugged. "I heard one of the pilots tell how it was their own SAMs that caused the damage."

"Sam? Sam who?"

"Surface to Air Missile, a heat-seeking missile, the size of a telephone pole. The missile homes on to the exhaust of an enemy jet, goes up the tailpipe, explodes there—*Bavroom!*" James made a loud exploding noise. "But if the pilot spots the missile in time, he can outmaneuver it. The gravity pull upsets the missile, makes it stall out. The missile then falls back down to the ground."

"I see," Claire said. She did—she saw a flaming telephone pole falling on top of a house, on top of a school filled with children.

"The missile carries a 350-pound warhead. It makes a pretty damn big explosion. It can tear apart a plane or a village, either one."

After James had left, Claire spent the rest of the holiday swimming alone in the pool.

Bavroom! She said to herself between laps and at regular intervals.

Bavroom!

Suk san wan krit sa mart—merry Christmas.

Sa wat dee pee mai—happy new year.

Suk san wan gert—happy birthday.

Choek dee—best wishes or good luck, Miss Pat said.

Siri telephoned; he wanted to speak to James. When Claire told him that James was away in Nakhon Phanom, Siri said he was calling to invite them to his brother-in-law Chanai's ordination.

"Oh, you mean your wife, Priya's brother?"

"No. Not Priya's brother."

"Your sister's husband?"

"Buddhist Lent is traditional time for a young man to enter priesthood." Siri did not explain.

Priya did not explain either. Claire and Priya were sitting in the back of the Land Rover, and James was driving. They were on their way to Wat Pak Nam. Wat Pak Nam was in Thonburi, on the other side of the Chao Phya River. Except for once on a floating market tour with the JUSMAAG officers' wives, Claire had never been. Thonburi was more rural than Bangkok. The houses looked older. They had large gardens, orchards of mango, pomelo, durian.

"Thonburi looks prettier," Claire leaned forward to say to James. "We should live in Thonburi."

"Too far," Priya said. "No shops."

"Many foreigners come to Wat Pak Nam to study," Siri half turned his big head to tell Claire. "Wat Pak Nam is famous for meditation teacher. He speaks good English."

"That's nice," Claire said, not looking at James.

Wat Pak Nam was large, modern, and built out of white stucco. Claire had imagined something else—a wooden temple, an old temple. Inside she knelt on the cement floor; she copied Priya and pressed her hands together in a *wai*. In front of her a brand-new life-sized bronze statue of a seated Buddha was draped with jasmine leis; joss sticks were burning at his feet. One of the Buddha's hands was raised in the teaching position, long index finger touching thumb. Next to the statue of the Buddha three priests were standing, chanting. Thin shafts of light fell on the folds of their orange robes. Idly Claire wondered which of the three priests spoke English. The oldest, the middle priest, she decided. When the priest saw Claire looking at him, he frowned. Embarrassed, Claire looked down.

Chanai, Siri's brother-in-law, lay like a bundle of cloth thrown in front of the three priests. His head was shaved and he was dressed entirely in white. Only the bare soles of his feet showed. The three priests chanted and sprayed him with holy water. One time the water also splashed Claire, stinging her cheek. Startled, Claire opened her eyes, and again the priest frowned at her.

The incense and jasmine leis smelled too sweet; the chanting made Claire sleepy, her head heavy. When Claire shifted her weight, her body swayed so wildly she was afraid she would fall over, and she was afraid to move again.

James was kneeling in front of her. There was a small sweat stain on the back of his shirt. The stain was shaped like a continent—Australia? Claire watched as Australia spread, changed shape. A new land mass formed along one side, a long peninsula. She watched the stain grow, grow to look like Thailand. She watched James raise a shoulder, twitch it—as if James could sense Claire's eyes on his back—then reach around with his hand, and scratch his back—scratch where Laos was.

Claire shut her eyes. The ceremony dragged on—interminable, unintelligible. The chanting swept over her in waves. The waves drowned out all thoughts, all possibility of thought. Claire felt herself sinking deeper and deeper. Resisting, she struggled to think of facts, dates, names—the name of the neighbors back home—*Wilson*—her mother's maiden name—*Davison*—her mother's birthday. She tried to pray.

Claire prayed that Jim Thompson would come back. Claire prayed that, one morning soon, a taxi would drive through the gate of his house and Jim Thompson would get out. Jim Thompson, Claire imagined, would be so pleased to be home that he would tip the taxi driver a lot—a hundred *baht*—triple the amount of the fare. *Mai pen rai*, she could hear him tell the incredulous driver, and *Once in a lifetime*, or words to that effect which the driver would not understand. Jim Thompson was carrying a small suitcase. He was neatly dressed in white silk trousers, a silk printed sport shirt. He looked well, he looked rested. Perhaps he looked a little thinner, but that was all right: he had wanted to lose weight—a pound or two.

Jim Thompson glanced around the garden—*his* garden. During the rainy season the plants had grown twice as tall, twice as lush. The purple orchids that had been placed around the sixth-century Dvaravati torso were in full bloom.

Yee, the servant, was squatting in the kitchen eating his breakfast of rice from a bowl. He would have heard the taxi drive up, and he would have put down his bowl and his chopsticks and gone to the door to see who was arriving at this early hour. Frowning, Yee was about to tell whoever it was that he was trespassing or that the house was not yet open to the public.

Then Yee saw who it was. Yee could hardly believe his eyes. Yee got down on his knees. With his hands Yee grabbed hold of Jim Thompson's silk trouser leg. *Nai! Nai!* he cried out, and Jim Thompson smiled and laughed. Jim Thompson even wiped a tear from his eye as he told Yee, in English, to get up off his knees and stop being so silly, and that, *yes, yes,* he was back.

Chanai stood up. He was just a boy—twelve or thirteen years old—but his face looked old. He bowed low to the three priests; one of the priests gave him a begging bowl. Then everyone stood up. Claire struggled clumsily to her feet. She felt stiff. Thirsty. *What time is it?* she wanted to ask. *And what day? Today? Yesterday? Or a day next week?*

On the way home from Wat Pak Nam, Claire sat in the back of the Land Rover with Siri.

"Tell me, Siri—Chanai looks so young—is Chanai your sister's husband's brother or is Chanai your brother's—"

"Claire, please, can you quit that!" James said.

In the front seat Priya was sitting next to James. Each time Priya said something—something Claire could not quite hear—to make her point or to emphasize a word, she placed her hand on James's arm, left it there. Priya's hand was slender and her nails were long and painted red. Each time, too, that Priya leaned over, her long dark hair brushed against James's shoulder as he was driving. Once when Priya was leaning over and her long dark hair was brushing up against James, a truck on the road in front of them started to make a turn without signaling. From the backseat, Claire called out:

"James! Watch out!"

The chances of the present king, King Bhumibol, who was born in Cambridge, Massachusetts, while his father, Prince Mahidol, was studying medicine at Harvard University, becoming king then were extremely slim . . .

For once Claire was absorbed in her reading at the British Library. For once she had no trouble imagining Prince Mahidol walking hand-in-hand with his pretty young wife, Princess Phraratanani, and their two small sons, a retinue of servants following them at a discreet distance, as first they crossed Harvard Square, then as they continued on down Eliot Street past the brick dormitories until they reached the banks of the Charles River. All of them would be dressed warmly in fur coats, fur caps, unused as they were to the New England cold, to the short dark winter days.

Between King Bhumibol and the throne stood any children King Rama VII might have, Prince Mahidol, his father, and Prince Ananda, his older brother. But Rama VII had no children, Prince Mahidol died in 1929, then King Rama VII abdicated, and Prince Ananda, who was still a student in Switzerland when he was crowned king in 1935, was killed under mysterious circumstances . . .

Did young King Ananda accidentally cut himself as he took his golden diamond-studded ceremonial sword out of its golden diamond-studded scabbard and die from lead poisoning? Claire wondered. Or was the teak and gold palanquin in which King Ananda rode not secured properly so, when it toppled off the elephant's back, King Ananda fell between the elephant's heavy legs and was trampled to death? Or worse still, like senile old King Taksin, was King Ananda placed inside a sack and then beaten to death with sandalwood clubs?

"Where do you keep the old newspapers?" Claire went over and asked the librarian from Melbourne, Australia. "Can I look? Newspapers from 1946?"

"1946? That's over twenty years ago." The librarian frowned. "What do you want those old newspapers for?"

"No reason, just curious. Oh, and next week when I go to the PX, I'll get you some more cigarettes," Claire said. "Which kind would you like this time? Regular or menthol?"

In the stacks of the British Library the newspapers were shelved in large piles. Yellow, old, the pages torn, in Claire's hands they crumbled nearly into ash. Probably the newspapers were biased, unreliable. Even so, Claire started looking through them.

"I don't believe them." Claire and James were arguing. "They never tell the truth!"

"They? Who are you talking about, Claire?" James had just come home from Nakhon Phanom. He had just put down his briefcase and taken off his cap; his red hair was just starting to curl around the damp ring made by the brim. "The truth about what?"

"The Thais. Everyone." Claire gestured toward the back of the house, to the kitchen. "The woman who stole my sauceboat. Noi, Prachi. What about my gold pin? It's still missing. Siri and Priya. Can you explain to me how Chanai is Siri's brother-in-law if he is not Siri's sister's husband and if he is not Priya's—"

"Claire, you're getting all worked up over nothing. The Thais are always claiming relationships that don't exist— aunts, uncles, cousins. It doesn't mean anything. It's just a term. A term of endearment."

"You call it endearment, I call it lying!" Claire shouted back at James. Upstairs, she slammed the bedroom door.

Geeve me ah kiece, Priya, leetal sisstah.

17

TWICE CLAIRE SWORE SHE SAW JIM THOMPSON.

The first time she was on her way to the photographer's studio on New Road, getting out of a samlor and paying the driver. Out of the corner of her eye she saw him turn and go down Oriental Lane. Not waiting for her change from the driver, she started to run after him.

"Mr. Thompson!" Claire called. "Jim Thompson!"

A woman carrying two heavy dangling baskets on her shoulders was walking toward her. The woman was half-blocking the narrow sidewalk. Claire hesitated for a moment; she could not make up her mind on which side to pass the woman.

"*Bpai nai?*" the woman with the baskets asked.

"Damn," Claire said.

Jim Thompson had slipped into the crowd. She had lost him.

Claire ran to the Oriental Hotel. Breathless, she rushed into the lobby. The lobby was cool, hushed. The ceiling fans whirred evenly above the polite hum of the receptionist talking on the telephone.

"Jim Thompson!" Claire ran shouting up to the desk. Her blouse had come untucked from her skirt and strands of hair had fallen into her face. "Did Mr. Thompson come in here?"

"Mr. Thompson? *Mai mi*—not here. Mr. Thompson—" Putting down the telephone and unsure how to finish, the receptionist blushed and turned away.

Nearly tame tropical birds flew back and forth in the open corridors. They perched on the upstairs balconies. In a corner of the lobby Claire saw a group of women sitting next to some potted plants, waiting. The women were fanning themselves with plastic palm leaves; the logo of an airline was printed on their fans.

Claire started to walk across the lobby to the bar—Jim Thompson might have gone in there. Perhaps she would find him sitting at a table in one of the rattan chairs, looking out at the boats on the Chao Phya River. He would have ordered himself a drink—a gin and tonic. Pulling up a chair, Claire would sit down next to him; she would order a gin and tonic too.

"Did I hear you say Jim Thompson?" One of the waiting women had stopped fanning herself and was walking toward Claire. "That must be us," she said. "We are waiting for a tour of his house."

"Honors, suits, flowers, jokers," Priya sang out happily. She had kicked off her high-heeled shoes and was sitting with her legs tucked under her on the sofa in the living room.

"How many are there?" Claire asked Priya. Card games, Monopoly, dominoes had never interested her; she preferred to read. Mah-jongg looked complicated, time consuming. Claire hoped she had not made a mistake asking Priya to teach her how to play the game.

Before settling herself down on the sofa, Priya had wanted

a tour of the house. Upstairs she looked inside James and Claire's bedroom, the guestroom, the bathroom. She opened closet doors, bureau drawers. Priya examined Claire's scarves, Claire's underwear. She picked up the photo of Jim Thompson in the Thai newspaper.

"Who is this?" Priya wanted to know. "Your boyfriend, Claire?"

"Jim Thompson. The American who disappeared."

"Oh, millionaire. I read about him in Thai magazine," Priya said. "I read how he was kidnapped by love-sick aboriginal woman. Sakai woman."

"A what kind of a woman?"

"Sakai hilltribe people stay hidden in jungle. You never can see them. But once you fall into Sakai's hands, magazine I read said, once they fall in love with you"—Priya was giggling—"they never let you go. It's true. I read about another man, wealthy man from Johore state who fell into hands of Sakai woman and never returned. Some Sakai women are quite beautiful," Priya continued. "I think man might prefer to stay and not try to escape alone in jungle."

Before leaving the bedroom Priya opened James's bureau drawer with the Smith & Wesson .44 magnum inside it, and Claire had called out, "Priya, watch out! The gun is loaded!"

Priya also wanted to know how much each item she was examining cost: the portable radio, Claire's hairdryer, a gadget for removing lint off clothes which Claire's mother had sent her and that Claire had never used. Claire offered the gadget to Priya, and, looking pleased, Priya put it in her purse.

Just as Claire and Priya were starting to play mah-jongg, Priya had picked up a bowl on the coffee table—a brown and white Sawankalok ceramic bowl. The bowl was old, cracked, Priya pointed out, frowning. She preferred new china, not secondhand stuff.

"Dots, bams, craks," Priya continued to sing out. "Object of game is to match them."

Deftly Priya dealt out the smooth ivory tiles and built a wall with the remaining ones. Priya's arms were slender and graceful, and it was hard for Claire to imagine Priya in the arms of Siri, her fat husband.

"Since this is your first time, Claire, I'll begin," Priya was saying. "One who begins is always called *East*."

"*East?* Does that mean I'm *West?*"

Priya shook her head. "No. In mah-jongg there is only East."

While James was in the bathroom—she could hear him singing above the splashing water—Claire was going through the clothes he had thrown into the laundry hamper the night before. First, James's khaki pants. The pants were wrinkled, the creases gone, the cuffs covered with dried mud; along the seam of the seat of the pants a dried sweat stain ran all the way up to the waistband. Claire turned the pockets inside out, held the pants upside down, shook them. A few coins fell out of one pocket; in the other pocket she found two wooden toothpicks, a matchbook, and a crumbled white napkin. Carefully Claire unfolded the napkin. Would she find a telephone number? lipstick? dried semen? She found nothing. On its cover the matchbook advertised the Bamboo Bar in Luang Prabang; inside only a few matches were left. Next Claire picked up James's shirt. She held the shirt up to her face, smelled it. The shirt smelled of gasoline and sweat and of James's deodorant. Inside the shirt's pockets she found a ball-point pen and a folded up newspaper clipping. Unfolding it Claire read:

An American pilot, the Thai copilot, and one Laotian crewman were killed when a DC–3 (Dakota) belonging to the Continental Air Service crashed shortly after takeoff at

Nakhon Phanom airfield about 7 a.m., Tuesday, according to a
delayed report reaching here yesterday. The American pilot was
identified as David Medina, the Thai copilot as Sanan
Thonamon, and the dead Laotian was unidentified. The plane
had left Nakhon Phanom on a regular cargo flight when the
accident occurred. Shortly after takeoff one of the twin engines
refused to work and the plane crashed, catching on fire. The
flames consumed the aircraft and the three men aboard before
the rescue party could reach the wreck, the report said.
Continental Air Service is an American concern on contract to
the Thai and American governments for transport of cargoes.
One of the officials based in Bangkok said that "this was the
first fatal crash since the company started operations in 1962."
The company has a fleet of 52 aircraft of various types—one-
engined Porters, twin-engined DC–3s and Dorniers. Details of
the crash will be sent to the Civil Aviation Board of Thailand.

James's white T–shirt was still faintly damp from his
sweat, there were yellowish-brown rings under the arms. His
underwear was quite clean.

Luang Prabang was not far from the Plain of Jars. Claire
looked it up in the atlas. A hundred klicks—she measured it
out with her fingers on the map—a hundred fifty at most.
When she asked James about the name Plain of Jars, he said
there really were jars, hundreds of large stone jars.

"Have you been?"

"No one knows where they came from," James answered.

"Like Stonehenge," Claire said. "Can we go one day and
take a look—I mean, look at the jars?"

"You must be joking," James said.

In the Thai script there are forty-four consonants, forty-eight
vowels, Miss Pat said. As usual, Miss Pat and Claire were sitting across from each other at the dining-room table.

Overhead the fan stirred rather than cooled the hot afternoon air. In the Thai script there are no punctuation marks,
no capital letters, Miss Pat reminded Claire. In the back of
the house Claire heard Noi's baby boy start to cry. In the
Thai script, the words are joined together in one long sentence with no space between them. Claire heard Prachi
shout. She looked over at Miss Pat; Miss Pat lowered her
eyes. A space, however, is left between the end of one sentence and the beginning of the next sentence, Miss Pat said.
Noi shouted back at Prachi. Then Claire heard a loud slap
and Noi's baby boy crying harder at the same time as Miss
Pat lowered her head and began to copy down the forty-four
consonants and the forty-eight vowels in the Thai script for
Claire to memorize.

"Prachi's been fooling around with my stuff," James complained to Claire. "The papers in my briefcase, my clothes,
the Smith & Wesson."

James had brought the gun downstairs.

"Prachi? Are you sure it's Prachi?" Claire looked up from
her book.

James opened the door and went out on the terrace.
Claire followed him.

"Prachi's been doing a much better job cleaning out the
pool," she said.

James was spinning the cylinder of the gun.

"Look, James, my hair isn't green anymore."

James clicked shut the cylinder, pointed the gun toward
the canal. "I should fire the sneaky bastard."

"James, please. No."

"See the dog floating in the canal—the dead dog?"

James cocked the gun, aimed it. The dead dog burst—
first the dog's legs, then the dog's head, then a lot of little

pieces rose a few feet out of the water into the air before they sank. There was a terrible smell.

Prachi, Lamum, and Noi, who held the baby boy with the silver net over his penis in her arms, had come around from the back of the house. They stood watching James. A woman Claire had never seen before was standing with them, standing next to Prachi. Instead of a sarong, the woman wore bright yellow pants. The woman was very young, very pretty.

"Prachi!" James called to him.

"You see this, Prachi?" James asked.

Prachi nodded. "*Nai*'s gun," he said.

"My gun, you're damn right!" James was nearly shouting. "And I don't want anyone touching it. I don't want anyone fooling around with it. This means you, Prachi. This means Lamum and Noi. This means everyone—the woman over there, whoever she is." James paused for breath.

"Noi's sister's—"

"I don't give a goddamn who she is. I don't want you touching my briefcase, my papers either," James was still nearly shouting. "Otherwise you can pack up your bags and get the hell out of here. You understand me, Prachi?"

Prachi was nodding again. He had gone bright red in the face.

Again James aimed the gun at the canal, again he fired it. This time there was only a spray of water as the bullet disappeared into the dirty *klong* water.

"Who was the woman? The woman in the yellow pants?" Claire wanted to know afterward. "Prachi's new girlfriend?"

18

"What's wrong?" James wanted to know. In bed, he got off Claire.

"Nothing." Still early in the morning and already Claire's body was drenched in sweat.

"Don't you feel well?" James persisted.

"No, I'm fine."

"You have your period?"

"No."

"You're not pregnant, are you?" James touched Claire's arm.

Claire shook her head, drew away her arm.

"Beats me then," James said, getting out of bed. "If you don't feel well, you should go and see Dr. Ammundsen."

"What for? To take up golf, to take up bridge?"

"To do what? What are you talking about, Claire?"

"Nothing. It's the heat."

James was in the bathroom. Claire could hear him flushing the toilet, splashing water, washing himself. Soon James would begin to sing.

* * *

"What does your husband do?" Claire asked the librarian at the British Library.

"He's in the construction business. He builds highways, roads. He's gone a lot, but I manage to keep busy." The librarian winked at Claire.

"I see." Claire looked away. She did—she saw roads with huge potholes, collapsed bridges, washed-out streets.

June 10, 1946. Ananda Mahidol, 20-year-old King of Siam, was found dead of a bullet wound yesterday in the royal palace, and twelve hours later the Siamese Legislature named his brother, Prince Bhumibol Adulyadej, 18, as the new king. The Siamese police director told an emergency session of the Legislature that the king's death was accidental, and that the bullet went through the center of his forehead.

In the stacks of the British Library, Claire was reading the newspapers that reported on King Ananda's death.

Often described as a reluctant monarch, King Ananda was boyish and diffident. His favorite occupations were playing his saxophone and driving his American-made jeep around the palace grounds. Also, a fancier of firearms, he always kept a gun by his side and liked to practice firing it. Several weeks ago, a thief stole his favorite Luger automatic and King Ananda had been very upset.

Claire had to turn the yellowed pages slowly, carefully, otherwise the twenty-year-old newspapers would crumble into dust in her hands. The more Claire read about the case, the less likely it seemed that King Ananda had committed suicide, and the more likely it seemed that there had been foul play.

The military regime which seized power in a bloodless coup last Sunday said it had arrested seven persons in connection with the slaying of King Ananda Mahidol. Those arrested were Chaliew Tradunros, secretary to the late king, and palace attendants, Buth Talmasasarin and Chit Sighasensa, and four women. Lieutenant General Phin Chunhawn, Deputy Supreme Commander of the Siamese army, said that Senior Lieutenant Vajarachi Siddhivjev, a secretary to Pridi Panomyong, was an eighth suspect in the assassination but that he had disappeared. "There is definite proof that his late Majesty was murdered," General Phin Chunhawn declared. General Chunhawn also said that the plotters' aim was to prevent the return of the King and to displace the constitutional monarchy with a republic. He said members of the wartime Free Thai movement, in which Pridi Panomyong was a leader, were involved in the plot. The plotters, General Chunhawn added, sought to use 40-millimeter antiaircraft guns delivered to Siam by the Allies during World War II.

The JUSMAAG officers' wives were climbing the narrow steep steps of Wat Arun, the Temple of the Dawn. The bits of glass and broken porcelain embedded in the cement of the temple caught and reflected the sun. Squinting, Claire wished she had brought along a hat.

"God, it's hot," the JUSMAAG officer's wife climbing in front of her said. "Don't look down," she also warned Claire.

"Wat Arun was built on site of Wat Jang. Palace and royal temple of King Taksin," the guide said between steps and between breaths. "King Taksin founded new capital of Siam in Thonburi."

"Wasn't King Taksin the one who was beaten to death with sandalwood clubs because no one was allowed to touch him?"

"Wat Arun is seventy-nine meters tall," the guide did not answer Claire. "Wat Arun was built by Rama II and Rama III. Before completion, builders ran out of Chinese porcelain, and Rama III called upon his subjects to donate broken china." The guide pointed to the tallest spire.

"I'd be happy to donate my china. Every plate, cup, and saucer I brought over with me is either cracked, broken, or chipped. The servants throw—" the JUSMAAG officer's wife in front of Claire was saying while behind her, Deirdre said, "Brad is keeping track. As of yesterday, he *sayud*, five hundred and ninety-nine U.S. planes have been lost over North Vietnam. Probably it's up to six hundred by now, six hundred and one planes, six hundred and two U.S. planes."

Hok roy saam, hok roy see, hok roy ha— Claire nearly missed a narrow steep step.

The guide said, "When we reach top, ladies, you will have beautiful view of all of Bangkok. Of all of countryside. From Wat Arun you will be able to see for many miles."

Polite particles, Miss Pat said, were placed at the end of each sentence. A male speaker used the word *krap*, a female speaker used the word *ka*.

Saam baht ka—Claire was forced to bargain.

Fie baht krap—the boatman held up five fingers.

They settled on four, and the boatman lowered the long-tail of his outboard engine into the dirty canal water. The lock situated under the bridge which crossed Pratoo Nam Market was open, and Claire was on her way to Jim Thompson's house.

Dead brown blossoms hung from the frangipani bushes. The garden path that led from the *klong* to the house was covered with twigs, dead leaves. The path had not been swept clean.

Jim Thompson's dogs began to bark. They barked as Claire got out of the boat and walked toward the house.

"Hello!" Claire called out. "Yee!" The dogs frightened her, and, allergic to them, they made her throat close, her nose itch.

"Yee! Anyone home?" Claire called out again.

Wearing a faded cotton *pakama* and looking thin and tired, Yee came out onto the terrace that was paved with seventeenth-century bricks from Ayuthaya. He put his elbows on the terrace wall; he leaned over, grinned at Claire. Unsure what to say to him, Claire said she was a friend—*peun*—of Mr. Thompson, she had been to the house before.

Chai chai—Yee called down to her. She should come in. He remembered all of *Nai* Jim's friends—*Sassy Peeton, Dloomang Gaboady, Lowbut Kangeely, Samset Maw, Bahla*—

Yee, Claire realized, was drunk.

Inside the house the shutters were closed, and the living room was dark. Claire could hardly see the U–Thong-style head of the Buddha, the head of the sun god, Suriya, of Siva, the statues of Ardhanari, Hari-Hara, the two wooden Burmese *Nats*; she could barely make out the outlines of the painted lacquered chests, the Bencharong bowls, the silk sofa cushions. The room smelled musty, unused; there were no flowers in the vases.

There was a faint rustle in the corner of the room—the cockatoo chained to his perch. Claire walked over and held out her arm to him. Just in time she drew her arm back. The cockatoo would have taken a chunk out of it.

From the drawing room Claire walked to the dining room. This time the table was not set with rare and valuable blue and white Ming china, gleaming crystal, and shining silverware; there was no sign of the elegant red silk napkins and place mats. Instead a stack of dirty bowls, a dish filled with *nam-plah*, the fetid fish sauce, a pot half-

filled with cold rice, a bottle of Thai whiskey had been left
on the table.

The whiskey was the color of water. When Claire took
a sip of it, the whiskey felt like fire going down her throat.
She could feel it burning a huge ragged hole in her
stomach, the same kind of hole, she imagined, that one
of James's special bullets—the ones he said explode on
impact—might make.

Holding the bottle of whiskey in one hand, Claire walked
around the room. She wanted to look at the paintings hanging on the walls. In the first painting Prince Vessantara was
giving away his white elephant. Prince Vessantara was tall
and thin, he looked like Yee. In the second painting Prince
Vessantara had given away all his possessions, and he was
walking in the woods with his wife and his two children.
Prince Vessantara's wife was slender and dark-haired—she
looked like Priya—and in this painting Prince Vessantara was
short and muscular, he looked like Prachi fishing out the
bougainvillea leaves.

Claire took another sip of whiskey. This time the whiskey
burned only a small hole in her stomach—a hole an ordinary
bullet might make.

Slowly Claire went around the dining room again. She
wanted to see if she could find what the artist had deliberately left out of the Prince Vessantara paintings. A roof? a
tree? a sauceboat? a gold pin in the shape of an artist's
palette?

From the dining room—the dogs nervously followed her,
their nails clicking on the polished teak floor—Claire went back
through the closed-up musty drawing room to Jim Thompson's
study. The study was dark and she turned on the light.

Putting the bottle down carefully on the desk so as not to
spill the whiskey, Claire picked up the bronze statue with a

dozen arms, Prajnaparamita, the goddess of wisdom. Then she picked up the other statue, Chanda-li, the destroyer of ignorance. Holding a statue in each hand, Claire weighed them again. Of the two, Chanda-li felt even heavier to her.

On the first page of the guestbook, April 3, 1959—the date the house was completed—there were several signatures in Thai. The signatures of priests no doubt. Slowly Claire turned the pages filled with names, drawings, light verse, until she reached the last page of names—Jim Thompson's last dinner party. There were a dozen signatures: Prince and Princess Chamlong, Brigadier General and Mrs. Black, Princess Chumbot, Dean Frasche, Liliane Emery, Philipe and Diane Baude, and, of course, James's and her own signatures, which Claire traced with her finger. Despite the heat, she shivered. She drank a little more of the whiskey. This time the whiskey did not burn, it merely felt warm. Claire drank some more.

The bedroom door was shut. Out of habit, Claire knocked. As she opened the door she heard a noise—the noise of someone getting up, leaving.

"Hello?" Claire stepped inside the room. "Anyone here?"

Claire caught a glimpse of a man's back. The man was wearing a sport shirt, white trousers. The man ran out onto the balcony. She could hear his hurried steps rushing down the balcony stairs.

"Yee?"

The yellow silk bedspread was partly thrown off the carved teak bed, exposing the wrinkled sheet underneath. Instead of being in a neat plumped-up row, the silk cushions at the head of the bed were untidily bunched together—two of the silk cushions were on the floor.

"Mr. Thompson?"

Claire glanced quickly around the room—the Chinese screen with painted glass panels, the wooden mouse house filled with little white porcelain mice, the gold votive plaques hanging on the walls, the tiger- and leopard-skin rugs on the polished teak floor—all looked in order.

"Mr. Thompson! Jim!" she called again.

Claire walked over to the bed, she picked the pillows off the floor, she straightened out the silk bedspread. The silk felt smooth and soft under her hands. All of a sudden, she felt a little sleepy, a little dizzy. Without thinking about it, she started to climb up—one knee then the other. She would lie down on Jim Thompson's bed for just a minute . . .

Then the dogs began to bark again. From his perch in the drawing room, the cockatoo started up a shrill screaming, and Claire could hear Yee walking toward the bedroom:

Sassy Peeton, Dloomang Gaboady, Lowbut—
Chaliew Tradunros, Buth Talmasasarin, Chit—

The remains of King Ananda Mahidol were removed from an urn today and X-ray photographs were made of the head to determine whether the bullet from a .45 caliber Colt automatic that killed him had gone in at the front or back of the skull. An official source said that an X-ray examination of the body of King Ananda Mahidol, who died of a gunshot wound in the palace on June 9, had proved conclusively that the bullet had entered the front of his head. X-rays of the skull showed that the bullet fragments from the front aperture had been driven inward and those in the back had been driven outward. The effects of .45 caliber bullets on a number of cadavers at the Sirarat Hospital were also studied. As a result, the medical men said they could estimate the distance from the head at which the gun was

*fired. This estimate was not made public but there were hints
that the distance was not great.*

Jim Jim Jim Jim Jim—Claire woke up in the middle of the
night.

"Sshhh. Drink this." James was holding out a glass of
clear liquid to her.

"Whiskey?" Claire pushed away James's hand.

"No, just water. And just a nightmare."

19

"A man was lying in his bed, I swear," Claire told James. "When I opened the door, the man ran out onto the balcony."

"What were you doing in Jim Thompson's house?" James asked. "Were you on another tour with the JUSMAAG officers' wives?"

"I only saw the man from the back. He was wearing a sport shirt, white pants. The same kind of clothes Jim Thompson always wore."

"The houseboy making out with his girlfriend, and how do you know what kind of clothes Jim Thompson always wore?"

In her next letter Claire's mother also mentioned Jim Thompson:

The other day I read an article in The New York Times about a man named Thomas who lives in Bangkok and who owns a silk store. The article said that he had a wonderful collection of Asian art and that his house is like a little museum. (Didn't you write how you go and sightsee with a group of women? So perhaps you've heard of this Thomas fellow.) It seems he disappeared while vacationing in Malaysia, and the story had such a sinister ring to it—it was not clear whether Thomas was a spy, a communist, or what. Anyhow, I imagine that Thailand is full of these shady characters—straight out of a Graham Greene novel. When I read the article out loud to your father, your father said the reason Mr. Thomas disappeared, most likely, was that he was a drug dealer!

Claire's mother's letter went on to describe how both she and Claire's father were looking forward to good weather on the Cape and to playing tennis. The summer before, Claire's mother wrote, there had been nothing but fog and rain. The letter ended with a P.S.: *Oh, I nearly forgot to tell you—do you remember the Wilsons who live down the street from us? I think you went to school with one of their children, Laura Wilson. In any case, her brother Andrew's plane was shot down last week. At first he was reported missing in action, but now the army has confirmed that he was killed. A real tragedy for them. I think he was their only son. I ran into Bettina Wilson in the street and she could hardly speak. She just waved to me in the saddest way. Poor woman.*

At night, lying next to James in the teak bed, when Claire could not sleep she would re-examine her day. As in a slow motion picture, she played the day back to herself—the electric whine of the overhead fan the whirr of a sixteen-millimeter camera. She began by going through the day in sequence: first thing when he woke up, James reached for Claire and they made love—some days James got on top of Claire, other days Claire got on top of James; afterward she washed, dipping in the cold water from the *klong* jar in the bathroom; they had breakfast together on the terrace— Claire had a cup of coffee, James ate a curried shrimp rice dish with the hot pepper sauce; they read the newspaper,

The Bangkok Post; they watched the woman bathe in the canal without exposing any bare flesh; then James left for work and Claire hailed a taxi boat to go to Pratoo Nam Market. After a while, however, restless or a little bored, Claire began to manipulate her day. She slowed down a frame or fast-forwarded it so that when Noi held up her baby boy to defecate in the canal, instead of wearing only the silver net over his penis, he wore clothes. Or Claire reversed it so that the bloated dog bobbing up and down in the water, stinking and ready to burst, was alive, shaking himself dry on land, a stick in his mouth. She zoomed in on the muscles on Prachi's back as, with his net, Prachi fished the bougain-villea and frangipani leaves out of the swimming pool; she made the muscles larger. Or Claire mixed things up further by fading out the dancing woman in the hula-skirt on Captain Ruengrit's Hawaiian shirt, focusing on a purple orchid blooming next to the Dvaravati-style torso in Jim Thompson's garden, replacing her smashed bowl with the valuable blue and white Ming bowl from Connie Mangskau's store; at the Pasteur Institute she shrank the king cobras until they were the size of the noodles in the snake handlers' bowls; she had the two soldiers with the woman in Pattaya give her a friendly wave from where they were sitting together on the beach, drinking beer and patting the honey bear; she found the pin in the shape of an artist's palette in the back of her bureau drawer, only, inexplicably, the pin had turned from gold to silver; the cargo inside the Dakota plane that crashed in Nakhon Phanom was hundreds of brown paper bags that, just as James was trying to pick them up off the runway, blew up into the sky like kites; and finally she missed completely with the too-heavy twelve-gauge shotgun the railbird that had the baby chicks.

Each night Claire became more and more adept at distorting images, tampering with scenes—and, anyway, she had done it before.

On a rainy day a long time ago, when she was twelve or thirteen years old and alone in the house on Cape Cod—Claire could not recall where her parents were, except that they were away for the entire afternoon—she had gone up to the attic. The attic was filled with old trunks, discarded things; the attic was stuffy, and Claire had opened a window. With the rain, there was also patchy fog. She could not see far out to sea or to the bell that marked the entrance to the harbor. On an impulse she climbed out onto the window ledge; as if the ledge were a horse, she sat astride it. Claire was wearing shorts and she pressed the wooden sill between her bare thighs. She started to rock and squeeze the sill between her legs, but it was uncomfortable; the wood was rough, and she soon loosened her grip. She let her legs dangle free. One leg was inside the attic; the other leg rested against the shingles of the house, outside in the rain. After a while the outside leg started to look different from Claire's other leg. First like a disembodied leg, then not like a leg at all. She could not name it. There it was, hers yet not hers. She did not dare touch it; she could not move it. Like the heavy clapper of the distant bell that she listened to, the leg hung there against the shingles of the house. Claire watched her sock sag with the damp, her white sneaker turn gray. She did not know how long she sat there; at the time, it felt like being dead.

On Sunday James invited Siri and Priya to the house. He was going to give Priya a swimming lesson in the pool, he said. He also asked Claire to fix Siri something special for lunch.

"I could open a jar of peanut butter."

Claire!" James was examining the label of a bottle of

California white wine that Claire had bought at the PX. "Siri and Priya are our friends, we have to pay back their hospitality."

Hok roy hok, hok roy jet, hok roy pat—

Sweating from the heat of the charcoal pits in the kitchen, Claire was basting another *gai* inside the aluminum box.

"Chicken," Claire said.

Six hundred six, six hundred seven, six hundred eight—

Siri was sitting on the terrace in the shade while James and Priya were in the pool. Claire could hear James and Priya splashing in the water. She could hear James calling out to Priya: "That's right, kick your legs out. Keep your chin up. Yes. Great! Now your arms. That a girl, Priya. Yes! Yes!"

Afterward, dressed in their best sarongs, Lamum and Noi served lunch. Wearing a shirt and long trousers, Prachi watched them as he went through the motions of cleaning out the pool with his net.

"You see me swim, Claire?" Priya asked her. "Now I swim like you."

"America aid no good. Queen Cobra Regiment receive single-barrel forty-millimeter antiaircraft guns that American soldiers don't use in World War II," Siri was complaining to James between mouthfuls of roast chicken. "Guns don't fire. Guns, I betcha, are thirty years old."

"That's nothing, Siri. Wait until you hear—" James started to say.

"The same kind of guns we gave the men accused of killing King Ananda," Claire said.

"Killing king who?" James said.

"King Ananda killed by communists. King Ananda killed by Pridi Panomyong," Siri said.

"Pridi who?"

"Pridi Panomyong was the leader of the resistance movement during World War II. He was one of the good guys, wasn't he, Siri?" Claire tried to explain.

"Claire, good chicken," James said.

"Pridi Panomyong friend of communists. Friend of Chinese communists," Siri said.

"Where you buy chicken, Claire?" Priya asked her.

"Pratoo Nam Market. Pridi Panomyong was a friend of Mr. Thompson's. Jim Thompson, the American who disappeared," Claire also said.

"Pratoo Nam Market very expensive. How much chicken cost?" Priya wanted to know.

"Jim Thompson friend of communists, too. Friend of Chinese commu—" Siri said.

"What I started to tell you, Siri—and I'm not giving away any big secrets—" James interrupted, "is how a couple of months ago some fancy Stanford engineer tried to make rain by dropping silver halide crystals into cloud formations from especially equipped C–130 cargo planes. Instead of falling on the Vietcong, six feet of rain fell on a Green Beret team. You can imagine how those guys must have felt—like goddamn drowned rats."

"Like the cow," Claire said. "The poor cow they were going to throw out of the plane."

"Cow? How much cow cost, Claire?" Priya asked.

Hok roy cow, hok roy sip, hok roy sip jet—

The next time Claire went to the Erawan Hotel and to Connie Mangskau's antique store, the door was shut, the blind on the other side of the glass was drawn. When she tried to turn the knob, the door was locked. When she went next door to the travel agency and asked the woman at the desk if she knew where Connie Mangskau was, the woman shook her head.

Connie Mangskau *mai mi*—not here.

King Bhumibol Adulyadej succeeded his older brother, Ananda Mahidol, in 1946. A year later, a bloodless coup marked the beginning of a military junta rule in Thailand. To combat communist aggression, Thailand joined SEATO and Field Marshal Pibul's foreign policy led to closer cooperation with the United States . . .

The books at the British Library were no longer piled as high on Claire's desk, but each time she opened and read a page, she had to begin all over again: *King Bhumibol Adulyadej succeeded his older brother, Ananda Mahidol, in 1946. A year later, a bloodless coup marked the beginning of a military junta rule in Thailand. To combat communist aggression, Thailand joined SEATO and Field Marshal Pibul's foreign policy led to closer cooperation with the United States.*

Tired, Claire could not concentrate. She could barely get through a few sentences before her mind wandered, her eyelids drooped: *In 1957, another coup brought Sarit Thanarat, Thanom Kittikachorn and General Prapas Charusathien to power; the trio abolished the constitution, dissolved parliament, and banned all political parties. They declared economic development the national priority; and gradually the three leaders came to control all the major financial, commercial, industrial and foreign enterprises in Thailand . . .*

Claire opened the photographer's screenplay instead. *Thailand is the color of holidays: green and red. The green stands for bamboo and rice paddies; the red stands for bougainvillea, hibiscus, the Flame of the Forest tree that blooms after the rainy season . . .* But the whirr of the overhead fan reminded Claire of bed. She yawned, she shut her eyes. She let the hot afternoon slip by.

In the twenty years Jim Thompson had lived in Thailand, or Siam as he no doubt preferred to call the country, he had made many friends. High-ranking officials, prime ministers, Thai princes and princesses, rich businessmen. With his engaging smile, his easy courteous manner, he was popular with the Thais, especially after he had revived the silk industry, made it so profitable and world-famous that King Bhumibol himself awarded him the Order of the White Elephant. Then Claire let her mind wander further back to the early days, the days right after the war, when little was known about Siam except that it was always hot and the people were gentle and smiled a lot, and except for in Bangkok, the roads were mud and the country was made up of rice paddies and impenetrable bamboo jungle unexplored still by foreigners. And she liked to think how during this time Jim Thompson and his important and wealthy friends were busy making plans—plans for democratic reform in Thailand. After all, wasn't the Prime Minister, Pridi Panomyong, a close friend? In those days Jim Thompson, Claire imagined, must have had easy access to the palace; he must have seen King Ananda drive the American-made jeep around the palace grounds, heard him play the saxophone, watched him shoot his Luger pistol. Right away Jim Thompson would have gotten the news of poor King Ananda's death. A suicide, the official announcement at first said—to save face. But the angle at which the bullet had entered the king's head made it impossible for King Ananda to have pulled the trigger himself. Claire could picture the blood-stained pillow but not the wide-open head. And what about the attendants—Chaliew Tradunros, Buth Talmasasarin, Chit Sighasensa? And the four women who were arrested? Were they summarily found guilty and shot in the head as well?

Then Claire started to think about what Jim Thompson was really like—she had heard enough rumors. Claire let her head drop on the photographer's screenplay—determined to marry the Akha girl wearing the headdress made out of silver coins, the Karen hilltribe man planned to kidnap her, thus forcing her parents to give their consent—and she mixed things up further. When Jim dropped out of the sky into Thailand, Claire was there first. She helped him fold his parachute, she brought him tea. Her hair was long, dark. She lived in a village. *Soon the war will be over,* she told him, *and you can take off your uniform.* It was blue with gold braid. Barefoot, Claire led Jim along a winding path; at night the stars were as bright as lights. Younger, Jim's face was unlined, fuller. *You speak beautiful English,* he told Claire. *My father is a professor,* she said. *He taught me English before I could read.* Claire wore an orchid in her hair, a rare species. She and Jim danced in the street, the whole village was celebrating. His arm around her waist, Jim was holding Claire in a tight embrace.

The librarian from Melbourne, Australia, startled her. "Are you asleep?"

20

BACK HOME, FALL WAS CLAIRE'S FAVORITE TIME OF YEAR. From her bedroom window, she could watch the leaves of the big maple in the backyard turn from green to yellow, then from copper to red. In Thailand, October marked the end of Buddhist Lent, not the beginning of a different season. In Claire's garden the bougainvillea, poinsettia, hibiscus bloomed all year long in vicious reds.

"Who was the woman?" Claire asked Prachi. She was spraying the roses in the garden with antifungal powder. Prachi was putting chemicals into the pool. "The woman who was here a few weeks ago. The woman in the yellow pants? Was she Noi's sister's—"

Prachi shook his head. "*Mai mi.*"

"I know she's not here, but what was her name?" Claire asked. "She was pretty," Claire continued. "Nearly as pretty as Noi."

Prachi did not answer.

"Is she your new girlfriend, Prachi? I bet you have a lot of girlfriends," Claire said. "How many girlfriends do you have, Prachi? Six hundred and twelve? Six hundred and thirteen? Six hundred and fourteen?"

After a while and after Prachi still did not speak, Claire said, "I don't know but something keeps eating away at these buds. Not a single rose has bloomed yet."

Claire, Miss Pat said, had progressed so well in the Thai language that she was ready to start translating—translating texts from English to Thai. Easy texts. She should begin with simple declarative sentences—sentences from magazines, sentences from guidebooks. Claire, Miss Pat also said, should choose the first sentence for their next lesson.

On March 6, 1962, the Rusk-Thanat Communique stated that the security obligations under the Manila Pact or SEATO—a regional collective security arrangement that included Australia, Britain, France, New Zealand, Pakistan, the Philippines, and the U.S.—were both individual and collective. In other words, the communique stated that the American obligation in the event of aggression did not depend on the prior agreement of all the other parties.

"Too hard. Too long." Miss Pat blushed and shook her head when she read what Claire had copied out of James's JUSMAAG handbook.

Now James kept his briefcase locked, but after only a few attempts Claire figured out the combination—030867—their wedding day. When she looked through James's papers, she was careful not to leave fingerprints and not to move them out of order. Along with a lot of handbooks, most of the papers were ordnance reports, troop supplies, blueprints for roads, for runways, for Claire-did-not-know-what, and she glanced through them quickly. Sometimes a single sheet of paper caught Claire's eye—a list of soldiers' names—most of the names were Thai or Laotian—an order form for cement blocks, steel rods, wire mesh. One time Claire found

a phone number scribbled on the outside of an envelope—
852928.

When Claire dialed the number, a Thai woman's accented
voice answered the phone:

Hero! Hero!

"Who's Will?" James had brought home the mail. Frowning,
he handed Claire a postcard. "Who's Lisa?"

The postcard had a picture of a smiling Oriental woman
with an orchid in her hair. The message read: *We are now
in*—the name of the town or the village or the rice paddy had
been blocked out by the censor—*meanwhile the jungle rot is
spreading from my feet to my*—that word too had been
crossed out, but not by the censor. *The orchid in the woman's
hair blooms once a day. Lisa sends love.*

Claire put Will's postcard in her bureau drawer next to
the newspaper clipping with the picture of Jim Thompson.
Taking the newspaper clipping out of the drawer, Claire
stared at the picture. Then, for no reason she could think of,
she put the picture to her lips.

Let me give you a kiss!

Afterward Claire sat down and wrote a letter:

*Dear Dr. and Mrs. Ling, I am taking the liberty of writ-
ing you in regards to the orchid plant that Jim Thompson
brought you when he came to visit in the Cameron
Highlands over the Easter weekend. (There was a newspaper article in the Bangkok Post last March or maybe it
was in early April, I no longer remember the exact date, by
a Mr. Perera, a reporter for the Bangkok Post, who was
on the same flight to Penang as Mr. Thompson and
who noticed the plant.) I later spoke to Mr. Perera's wife
who confirmed this and who also informed me that the*

*plant was a rare orchid species called a Javanese
Dendrobium and that the plant only blooms once every few
years. I know that it has been several months since Mr.
Thompson's disappearance, but I was hoping that you
would be able to tell me if the orchid, the Javanese
Dendrobium, has in fact bloomed yet. I have enclosed a
self addressed envelope for your convenience. Thanking
you in advance for the information, I remain yours
truly . . .*

Claire rewrote the letter several times before she was satisfied with it and before she tore it up.

Each time Claire crossed Noi on the stairs, Noi smiled; even
if Noi was carrying the two heavy cases of bottled water to
their bedroom, Noi smiled at Claire.

"Did you hang up my ironed blouses on hangers and fold
Nai James's ironed shirts in the drawer?"

"*Wan tu slii.*"

"Is Lamum your mother and is Prachi the father of your
baby?"

"*Fo fie see.*"

"Was the young woman wearing the yellow pants who
was here the other day Prachi's new girlfriend?"

"*See, thaivin, ait.*" Noi was still smiling.

"I read your screenplay," Claire told the Thai photographer when she went back to his studio next to the post office
on New Road. "I liked it—a Siamese version of *Romeo and
Juliet.* Also I want to show you something." Claire handed
him the passport photographs. "The photos you took are not
of me."

The photographer looked at the photos, looked at Claire.
His face turned red. "I must have mixed you up with

another *falang* lady who came to the studio the same day," he said. "I remember now, she was a French lady. The French cultural attaché's wife." The photographer's face got redder. "Please, forgive me. I'll give back your money."

As again the photographer adjusted the backdrop, his camera, to take another picture, Claire started to laugh. She laughed so hard, tears streamed down her face. She laughed so hard she had to sit down. She had to lie down. People walking outside in the street heard her. A few of them stopped to look in at her. One man brought Claire a glass of hot tea.

Ha ha ha ha ha ha ha ha

Claire was laughing so hard she spilled the tea.

After the photographer had developed and printed the pictures, Claire was still laughing.

Ha ha ha ha ha ha

On the way to the American Embassy, in the samlor, Claire opened the envelope with the two sets of photographs and looked at them again.

Ha ha ha ha ha ha

She held up a set of photographs in each hand and compared them: in one Claire's hair was flat, straight; in the other the French cultural attaché's wife's hair was smooth and in place. Claire's eyes were shut and her mouth—she was trying not to laugh—was twisted in a grimace; the French cultural attaché's wife was looking straight into the camera, her smile was candid and serene.

Ha ha ha ha ha ha ha ha

The French cultural attaché's wife wore a tailored blouse, open at the collar; she wore a string of pearls. Claire was wearing a T–shirt.

Ha ha ha ha ha

When the samlor driver turned around in his seat to look

at Claire and see what she was laughing at, he nearly ran his
samlor into an overloaded bus.

Ha ha ha ha

"Which of these two women looks more reliable?" Claire
waved a set of photographs in the air and shouted at the samlor driver. "Which of these two women looks prettier?"

Suay mahk.

Ha ha

At the American Embassy the marine guard waved her
right in without looking at her old passport which had
expired. The American consul, a young woman, was in a
hurry. She handed Claire the new one without looking at
either the passport or at her. "Don't forget to sign it," was
all the consul said.

Ha ha ha ha

Everything made Claire laugh.

Or nearly.

*During the twenty years as the ninth ruler of the Chakri
dynasty, King Bhumibol and his beautiful wife, Queen Sirikit,
have proved themselves worthy . . .*

Ha

*. . . experimental rice fields, dairy farms, programs for arti-
ficial rainmaking . . .*

Ha

. . . improving the lot of the northern hilltribes . . .

Ha ha

*. . . as a result, the Thai monarchy is stronger now than at
any other period since . . .*

Ha

At the British Library, Claire had only a few pages of Thai
history left.

* * *

On her way home at the PX Claire bought a bottle of California white wine, a carton of menthol cigarettes, then she went over to the section of the store that sold children's clothes, children's toys.

"Hi. What are you looking *foh* over here?" a southern voice asked. Deirdre, the JUSMAAG officer's wife, was pushing a shopping cart full of canned goods.

"Nothing. I'm buying something for my nephew," Claire answered, holding up a little T–shirt with *U.S. ARMY* printed on it.

21

"*F*OH!*"

"Fore!" Claire shouted, copying Deirdre.

See!

Deirdre had asked Claire to play golf with her. Claire had accepted. Easier to say *yes*, she told James, and James said: "Good for you to get your nose out of a book and do something else for a change."

"Keep *yoh haid* down, keep *yoh ahs* on the ball, and swing," Deirdre instructed Claire.

Claire swung the wood club and a clump of grass flew up.

"*Lahk* this." Deirdre showed her.

"What I *lahk* about golf is I could be anywhere," Deirdre also told Claire, "the Netherlands, South America, North Carolina—"

"Don't you like Thailand?"

"*Thai*land could be worse, I guess." Deirdre pronounced it *Thighland*. "What about you, Claire?"

"It's too hot." Claire shrugged. "But it's interesting—the history, the culture, the customs."

"I *lahk* the *Thai* dancing," Deirdre answered. "The silk, too, is *nahce*."

The next time Claire swung, she hit the ball on its side, and it rolled a few feet off the tee.

"There, you've nearly got it. Don't forget to keep *yoh haid* down. But if you think about it," Deirdre continued, "the silk industry was started by an American—the American who disappeared a few months ago—Jim what's-his-name."

"Jim Thompson."

Claire and Deirdre were walking down the fairway together. The caddy, a young Thai boy, was carrying Deirdre's golf bag. Since this was Claire's first time, Deirdre had offered to share her clubs with Claire.

"That's *raht*. Jim Thompson. Before Jim Thompson came to *Thai*land, silk weaving was just a cottage *industrah*."

Deirdre hit her second shot a few yards off the first green. "Good shot," Claire told her.

"Not only people *lahk* Jim Thompson, but if it weren't for us Americans, who knows what *Thai*land would be *lahk* now," Deirdre said as she took the nine-iron the caddy handed her.

"Hogtied," Claire answered. "We Americans have the Thais hogtied."

"Hogtied?" Deirdre stopped midswing. "What are you talking about, Claire? The *Thais* should be *gryteful* to us."

"That's what everyone says. That's what James says too. But it's not true." Claire went on. "The American presence in Thailand has eliminated any hope that the Thais can reach any kind of agreement with their neighbors"—which book had she read this in? where had she heard this?—"Burma, Laos, Cambodia, Vietnam, even North Vietnam."

"An agreement with North Vietnam? Claire, have you gone *cryhzy*?"

The next time Claire swung at the ball, she connected with it squarely. Only, at the last moment, she lifted her head and the ball sliced to the left and caught a caddy, who was walking down the opposite fairway carrying another golfer's bag, in the head. The caddy dropped to the ground as if he had been shot.

Claire took the caddy in a taxi to the Seventh Day Adventist hospital on Pitsanuloke Road. He had regained consciousness but there was a big lump on his forehead where the golf ball had struck him. At the hospital Claire and the caddy had to wait nearly an hour before a doctor could see them. Sitting next to Claire, the caddy, a boy of fourteen or fifteen whose only words of English were *too lood, fie ilon, puttel, gleen,* kept his head on his knees and moaned. He kept moaning when, finally, the doctor examined him. The doctor was Scottish and did not seem concerned. He examined the caddy's pupils to see if they were dilated, listened to the caddy's heart, took the caddy's blood pressure and pulse; eventually he pronounced the caddy all right.

"But he seems to be in a lot of pain. How about giving him something—some aspirin?" Claire said.

"Aspirin?" The Scottish doctor shook his head. "Aspirin isn't going to do him any good. I'd give him some *baht*— quite a lot of *baht*."

"Give him what?"

"About ten thousand *baht* should make that moaning stop."

"Oh, money."

By the time Claire got home the sun had nearly set behind the Flame of the Forest tree that stood by their garden gate, and she was tired. On the dining-room table, James had left her a note. The note said that he was sorry he could not wait to say goodbye but he had to go up to Nakhon Phanom for two days. James signed the note: *Much love to the new 1967 Thai women's open golf champion!* And by the time Claire went upstairs to change into her bathing suit and came back down again, it was dark.

Floating on her back in the pool the way James did, Claire felt something against her leg. She drew her leg back. Only a leaf. When she turned over and started to swim, she felt something else brush against her arm. Another leaf. The pool was filled with floating dead leaves.

"Prachi!" Claire yelled.

Claire climbed out of the pool and called to Prachi again. "*Mem?*" Noi came.

"Where's Prachi?"

Noi ran around to the back of the house.

Noi's baby started to cry. Then Claire heard another sound, the sound of a horse whinnying.

At last Prachi appeared. He was still tying his *pakama* around his waist. Instead of combed down, his hair was standing straight up. He looked as if he had just woken up.

"Prachi, what's going on here?" Claire asked him. "As soon as *Nai* James goes away to Nakhon Phanom, the pool is full of leaves."

Prachi shrugged his muscular bare shoulders and grinned.

"And what's back there? A horse?"

Prachi was still grinning.

"Prachi, I don't want a horse in my—" Claire started to say, but Prachi was not listening to her. Prachi had picked up his net and was flailing the water with it in a vain attempt to scoop the leaves out of the pool in the dark.

After dinner Claire sat alone in the living room drinking another glass of white wine—the California white wine she had bought at the PX and the same wine she and James had drunk with Siri and Priya for lunch. She was reading a magazine:

So far, the U.S. has lost 689 planes. Their pilots either "buy the farm" or end up at "the Hanoi Hilton." The three out of four who do get back and manage to complete 100 missions win membership in an elite club that now numbers in the hundreds. When a pilot hits the magic mark, his fellow pilots and flight mechanics roll out the red carpet for his return, give him a rousing, horn-honking parade of fire trucks and maintenance vehicles. In turn, he provides a bottle of champagne, then forks out a month's combat pay for drinks all around. One of the favorite drinks is a MIG–21, a paralyzing concoction consisting of three jiggers of Scotch and one jigger of Drambuie on the rocks.

Claire put down the magazine and went to the refrigerator. She got some ice and poured herself a glass of Scotch. Then, since she could not find any Drambuie in the cupboard where James kept the liquor, she substituted brandy for it. Why not? The drink might put her to sleep quickly.

Claire woke up to an unfamiliar sound, but a sound she had long imagined—the sound of *kemoys* slashing away downstairs at the window screens with their curved and razorsharp knives. Her heart pounding, Claire got out of bed and put on her robe. She took James's Smith & Wesson .44 magnum out of the bureau drawer.

She tiptoed to the top of the stairs.

"Prachi."

Claire stood listening.

"Prachi?" she whispered.

The sound Claire heard was no longer the sound of *kemoys* slashing the window screens; now it was a different sound and it was coming from outside the house. From the garden. Holding her robe shut with one hand and the heavy pistol with the other hand, Claire slowly started down the stairs.

"Prachi?" she called again.

The sound was getting louder and more distinct—a thrashing, splashing sound—and it was coming from the swimming pool. Cautiously Claire opened the door and stepped out on the terrace.

Claire would never remember letting go of her robe to hold the Smith & Wesson .44 magnum steady in both hands the way James had shown her; she would never remember taking the Smith & Wesson off safety, cocking it, aiming it; she could never remember pulling the Smith & Wesson's trigger; but as long as she lived she would always remember the bright orange flame that leapt unexpectedly from between her hands, burnt a straight line through the dark fragrant night, then, without a single spark, went out.

"Prachi!"

Instead of Prachi, there was a horse. The horse kept whinnying—a high-pitched frenzied whinny which sounded like a woman screaming—as the horse kept churning around the pool in a frantic circle. The horse held his wet head rigid out of the water. His eyes were rolled back, only the whites showed. The horse's nostrils were flared and bloody, his yellow teeth bared.

"Prachi!" Claire screamed.

Wrapped in faded sarongs, Lamum and Noi came running from the back of the house; Noi was holding the baby boy in her arms, he was wearing the T–shirt with *U.S. Army* printed on it. Lamum's long gray hair was not tied up the way it usually was but hanging down, thin and loose. Noi started to cry, loud wracking hiccupy cries, and Lamum patted Noi's arm trying to calm her.

Soon after, the neighbors were in the garden. The man

who collected orchid plants on the balcony next door had
filled a bucket with grain and placed it by the shallow end of
the pool. Police cars came with their sirens and flashing blue
lights that lit up the bougainvillea, hibiscus, sweet-smelling
frangipani bushes and the roses that never bloomed. A man
from the Pasteur Institute drove up in a tow truck with a har-
ness dangling from it.

First, they got the horse out of the pool. Then, just as the
sun was coming up, they got Prachi out of the pool—the blue
of the swimming pool had turned brown, manure patties
bobbed up and down on the still agitated water.

When Prachi was laid out on his back on the grass, Claire
heard the faint jingle of bells. Prachi was wearing the baby
gibbon's collar around his wrist. Before his face was covered
with a *pakama*, Claire had just enough time to see how the
bullet had entered Prachi's mouth and shattered his perfect
straight white teeth, how the bullet had exited through
Prachi's chin, then how the bullet had reentered Prachi's
chest and exploded there, making a hole as big as James's fist.

22

CLAIRE MUST HAVE TELEPHONED SIRI BECAUSE IN WHAT seemed to her only a few minutes Siri was there. Claire saw Siri heave himself out of the cramped backseat of a samlor. Siri was all dressed up, wearing a long-sleeved shirt and a tie. Instead of going to speak to Claire, Siri first went to speak to the policemen. Siri and the policemen spoke for a long time. Claire saw the policeman in charge take off his cap and wipe his brow with a white hankerchief as the morning sun, hot already, shone on them.

Claire was still in her robe and nightgown—only someone had taken the Smith & Wesson .44 magnum out of her hand. Lamum and Noi, too, in their faded sarongs, had not moved far from the swimming pool—Noi was still holding the baby boy wearing the T–shirt with *U.S. ARMY* printed on it. One of the policemen had staked the horse, a little brown horse more like a pony, with the clothesline, and, after rolling over on the ground several times, the little brown horse was eating the leaves of the hibiscus and frangipani bushes.

Then an ambulance arrived. The driver and the attendant picked up Prachi's body off the grass and put him on a canvas stretcher. Again Claire heard the faint jingle of bells—or she imagined it. The driver and the attendant placed the canvas stretcher inside the ambulance. When they slammed shut the ambulance door, Noi started to cry again. By this time most of the neighbors had left, and the man who collected the orchids on the balcony next door had taken back his bucket full of grain.

Afterward Claire must have gone upstairs to bathe and to get dressed—she even washed her hair. When she was dressed, she sat on the unmade bed and waited.

Neither Noi nor Lamum came up.

Siri telephoned JUSMAAG. Claire heard Siri ask someone to contact James, to tell James to come home right away—an emergency, Siri shouted into the receiver. Also, Siri might have called Dr. Ammundsen—but Claire did not think so. Midmorning the doctor drove up to the house. Claire happened to be looking out the bedroom window and she saw an unfamiliar blue car; she saw one of the policemen who had stayed behind put his head through the car window, then open the garden gate. Dr. Ammundsen let himself into the house and came up the stairs. Dr. Ammundsen did not say much. Only when Claire started to unbutton her blouse, Dr. Ammundsen told her to keep it on. This time he gave Claire a shot of Miltown.

Still, neither Lamum nor Noi came up.

From time to time Claire heard the sound of pots and pans in the kitchen, she heard the sound of something being dragged across the floor coming from the back of the house— from where Lamum and Noi and Prachi slept. One time she heard Noi's baby boy start to cry, then, almost immediately, Noi's baby boy stopped. Another time Claire heard the little brown horse whinny.

Once, she could have sworn—or perhaps Claire dreamt this—she heard Miss Pat's voice.

Hok roy pairt sip cow, hok roy cow sip, hok roy cow sip nung, hok roy cow sip song—

The telephone rang several times, but Claire did not answer. A policeman in the living room or else Siri, if he was still there, answered it because the telephone also stopped ringing.

A few times, too, Claire was tempted to call Noi; but she didn't.

When James finally got home it was afternoon. Claire almost bumped into him in the upstairs hall—she had just opened the bathroom door.

"Thank God!" James said. He took Claire in his arms. "When I first heard something had happened, I thought something had happened to you."

Claire started to cry.

"James, you should have seen Prachi—" she tried to say. "Poor Prachi's face. Poor Prachi's teeth—"

"Sshhh, I know. An accident," James said.

James sat beside Claire on the unmade bed. He put his arm around her shoulders.

"Not your fault, Claire. You want anything? Some water?"

Claire shook her head.

James said something else that Claire did not understand but which, to her, sounded like *Cameron Highlands.*

"You know what, James?" she said to him after a while.

"No. What?"

When she spoke, her words were slow, slurred, her voice did not sound like hers. "I've been thinking. I've been thinking about Jim Thompson."

"Jim Thompson? What does Jim Thompson have to do with any of this?"

"We kidnapped him."

"How do you mean *we*?"

"We. The U.S. government."

"Claire, you're upset. You're not making sense. Why would we want to kidnap Jim Thompson? Jim Thompson is an American." James took his arm from around Claire's shoulders; he ran his hand through his hair trying to comb down the red curls. "You want some whiskey?" he said.

Claire started to cry again.

The Thai police took the Smith & Wesson .44 magnum as evidence. The next day, when James tried to get the gun back, the police denied having it. When Siri made a special trip to the police headquarters and tried to convince the police to return the Smith & Wesson—Siri offered them money—again the police denied ever taking the gun. According to the police, James's gun had simply disappeared.

Lamum and Noi left without warning, without saying good-bye. They left without collecting their last month's pay.

"Noi!" Claire called out the next morning.

"Noi!" Claire went around to the back of the house, to the kitchen and to where Lamum and Noi slept. No one was there, and the rooms were swept clean. Everything—the straw mats that Lamum, Noi, the baby boy with the silver net over his penis, Prachi, and God-knew-who-else had slept on, the cooking utensils, all their meager possessions, including all the stuff Lamum and Noi collected, the cardboard boxes, the hangers, the bottles—had disappeared.

"Noi! Lamum!" Claire called out again, louder.

The little brown horse raised his head, whinnied. He was still staked to the ground, the clothesline caught around his front legs, he was almost hobbled in place. He had eaten

all the hibiscus and frangipani leaves within his reach—he
had even eaten the large messy banana leaves.

"Goddamn horse," Claire said.

"Who would ride a horse into a swimming pool?" James
said over and over again like a refrain. He shook his head. "I
can't imagine how Prachi got the horse in the pool in the first
place. Prachi must have been drunk. Drunk out of his mind."
To prove his point James brought out the bottle of Scotch.
The bottle of Scotch was half empty. "The imported French
brandy." James also showed Claire. "Prachi must have helped
himself to that too."

"You should have seen poor Prachi's teeth," Claire said
again.

The house was shuttered and closed, the outdoor furniture
brought inside. On the lawn there were tire ruts where the
police cars, the tow truck from the Pasteur Institute and the
ambulance had driven in and parked. From the outside the
house looked as if, like Lamum and Noi, James and Claire
had already left. The night before, someone heaped garbage
from the *klong* on their terrace. A dead dog? Claire wanted to
know, but James did not answer. James swept away whatever
the garbage was, but Claire thought she could still smell it.

*A body is different. A body should not be hard to find
in the jungle. Vultures fly over it. Animals are attracted by
the smell.*

Also, someone had stolen Prachi's net or else one of the
policemen had taken it as more evidence, and no one had
cleaned out the pool yet.

Upstairs, Claire was packing. Over the whirring of the
fan she could hear James and Siri talking downstairs. James
was explaining how it was all arranged: Claire would go
home, and, until his contract was up in a few months, James

would rent an apartment in the JUSMAAG complex; from now on he would be away in Nakhon Phanom a lot more anyway. Although clearly an accident, you never could tell for sure—James voice droned on and on—a relative of Prachi might decide to prosecute. In which case, according to Thai law and according to what he had heard, Claire, until she was proved innocent, would have to go to jail.

"A Thai jail," Siri said.

"You know, Siri," James was talking about something else. "I still feel sick about the Smith & Wesson. I've never owned a handgun like it. I'd do anything to get it back. Tell me again the word in Thai for gun—*peun?*"

"No, *peun,*" Siri said the word differently. "*Peun* means friend."

"*Peun,*" James repeated.

Siri said something that Claire did not catch.

King Ananda

"I know. Policemen are the same the world over," James said.

Tired, Claire shut her eyes. She had looked at the Thai newspaper clipping with the photo of Jim Thompson standing in front of his store on Suriwongse Road so many times she could picture him exactly. Not only could Claire picture him exactly, she could picture how, several months ago when she first arrived in Thailand, Jim Thompson had taken her arm to walk back from his study; she could picture exactly how Jim Thompson had smiled at her from where he was sitting at the head of the table and how he had promised to show her the rest of his house; she could also picture how he must have sat in the plane during the bumpy flight to Penang holding the Javanese Dendrobium in his lap; how at the last minute Jim Thompson decided to get a haircut in the hotel barbershop; and how he told Connie Mangskau that it did not matter to him and he would ride in the taxi with the man and the woman—poor woman!—who had her arm in a sling. Claire could picture almost everything up until she pictured how Jim Thompson was sitting outside on the terrace of the Moonlight Bungalow while Dr. and Mrs. Ling and Connie Mangskau were inside the house napping. Jim Thompson, she imagined, took off his jacket—one of those light blue and white striped seersucker jackets—and draped it over the back of the chair—a deck chair with wooden slats, the kind that used to be on ocean liners. He left his cigarettes, his Zippo lighter, inside one of the pockets of his jacket—he was trying not to smoke so much. In another pocket he kept the bottle with his gallbladder medicine. He had taken a tablet that morning; he would take another tablet again later. He was looking through a book—no, a catalogue of the Lings' antiques. Thumbing through it, something caught his eye; he stopped to read the caption: *Jar; Laotian; 15th century; Height 2.6 meters; from Plain of Jars. A thick coarsely crackled—* He looked up. Had someone called his name? As he stood up, the deck chair scraped against the flagstones on the terrace. Slowly Jim Thompson started down the gravel path in the direction of the rose garden. His hand extended, a man walked up to meet him. The man was big, huge—*Preebie? Pridi?*—the man looked like Siri. Was the man holding something in his hand? The afternoon sun was shining in Jim Thompson's eyes; he was only able to make out a dark object—a statue? a bowl? a . . .

No use saving the newspaper clipping with the picture of Jim Thompson. By now Jim Thompson, Claire was certain, was dead. Like Prachi, Jim Thompson probably had been shot in the head.

She knew what his wide-open head would look like.

"I don't think she knew what she was aiming at."

Downstairs Claire could still hear James's voice. "Ironic, too, since I was the one who showed her how to shoot. I was the one who told her to aim for the chest, not the head. And weird if you consider the path of the bullet, I've never seen anything like it—going in Prachi's mouth, then coming out—"

Claire took Will's postcard out of her bureau drawer. Will, she imagined, was dead as well.

"Oh, and the horse, Siri!" Claire heard James say as if he remembered all of a sudden. "What shall I do about the goddamn horse?"

"Don't worry, James," Siri answered James. "I know someone who raises horses. He'll take horse for you. No charge."

Before Claire left Bangkok she had to go to the police station. As a precaution James asked Siri to go with them. Siri, James told Claire, could translate for her. Siri's presence, however, proved unnecessary. Claire understood the question. In the Thai language, as Miss Pat had said, the context made the meaning clear to her:

Koon ying peun pai dooy mai dai kit?

EPILOGUE

Leaving the rice paddies behind, the plane's engines droned louder, straining a bit as the plane started to climb. Looking out the window, Claire watched the landscape below her unfurl into jungle, unmapped and patternless, without a sign of the hilltribes who lived there: the Akha, Yao, Meo, Karen, Lisu, Lahu, Sakai, and the Phi Thong Luang—the Spirit of the Yellow Leaves, except all the leaves in Thailand were green—the most elusive of the hilltribes. In vain Claire searched for a road, a plume of smoke, while all around her the sky remained cloudless, a constant blue, as the plane fitfully plunged through.

The plane was full of men going home. The men were rowdy and noisy. Several of them walked up and down the aisles—the stewardesses tried half-heartedly to get them to sit down—holding drinks and calling out to each other across the row of seats. One of the men stopped in front of Claire's seat; he leaned down to speak to her.

"Sweetheart, are you going home on leave or are you going home for good?"

Claire hesitated. "For good," she said.

"I'll drink to that." He stood over Claire and raised his glass. Some of the liquid in his glass—whiskey or beer—spilled on Claire's dress.

Claire raised her glass of Coca-Cola.

"Be happy," the man told her as he continued his unsteady way down the aisle. "You're alive!"

Claire brought several books to read on the plane. One of the books her teacher Miss Pat had given her as a goodbye present. The book was for schoolchildren and illustrated—the cover was worn, some of the pages were torn, many passages had been marked and underlined. Miss Pat told Claire that she knew that Claire liked antiques, secondhand things, and the book—stories about the Thai gods and goddesses—was easy to read, and a souvenir. During the long flight home, Claire, Miss Pat promised, would have plenty of time to find out that the reason Brahma grew five heads was to keep his beautiful wife Sarasvati, the goddess of learning and the arts, from escaping his amorous gaze; Claire, Miss Pat also promised, could take hours and hours to discover how Vishnu in the guise of a wild boar single-handedly saved the earth from drowning in the sea; Claire could spend all day and yet a whole other day, Miss Pat predicted, learning exactly how the monkeys helped Rama save his wife, Sita, by building a bridge across the ocean.

But Claire never opened a book. She had read enough Thai stories, and already, before they even started crossing the Pacific, she guessed what that bridge the monkeys built to save Sita looked like—one of those shaky rope bridges that gave her vertigo. Instead, Claire pulled down the window shade and shut her eyes.

The flight home took over twenty-four hours, and instead of putting her watch forward, Claire had to put her watch back one hour, then two, then four hours. Also this time they were flying east, toward the sun, and it was always the same bright day.